D0323533

Cannibal

ELMER HOLMES BOBST AWARDS
FOR EMERGING WRITERS

Established in 1983, the Elmer Holmes
Bobst Awards in Arts and Letters are pre-
sented each year to individuals who have
brought true distinction to the American
literary scene. Recipients of the Awards include writers as varied as Toni Morrison,
John Updike, Russell Baker, Eudora Welty,
Edward Albee, Arthur Miller, Joyce Carol
Oates, and James Merrill. The Awards were
recently expanded to include categories de-
voted to emerging writers of fiction and po-
etry, and in 1994 the jurors selected win-
ners in each category, Terese Svoboda for
her novel, Cannibal, and Alice Anderson
for her collection of poems, Human Nature.

Cannibal

terese svoboda

NEW YORK UNIVERSITY PRESS • NEW YORK AND LONDON

NEW YORK UNIVERSITY PRESS
New York and London

Copyright © 1994 by New York University

All rights reserved

Library of Congress Cataloging-in-Publication Data
Svoboda, Terese.
Cannibal / Terese Svoboda.
p. cm.
ISBN 0-8147-8012-1
I. Title.
PS3569.V6C36 1994
813'.54—dc20   94-34305
                                 CIP

New York University Press books are printed on acid-free paper,
and their binding materials are chosen for strength and durability.

Book design: Jennifer Dossin

Manufactured in the United States of America
10 9 8 7 6 5 4 3 2

To the Nuer, those who have not yet starved.

ACKNOWLEDGMENTS

I am deeply grateful to Amy Hempel, Willy Kelley, Sondra Spatt Olsen, Robert Levy, Shelly Silver, Pat Heller, Gillian Walker, and Mary Stewart Hammond who read pieces, and at times, whole versions of this in manuscript over the years. I can still see them shaking their heads, one way or another. But none of them read it as often as Steve Bull, who didn't go to Africa.

I have also been blessed by residencies at Yaddo, Mac-Dowell, Ossabaw, the Writer's Room, and several stays at J. Laughlin's Meadow House where, unbeknownst to him, I took license. Gordon Lish and his class furthered that license.

And thanks to my father, Frank Svoboda, for being original.

Cannibal

He doesn't look at it. I can't not look but he won't look. Maybe because I'm female and that's why. It's a female who walks some feet ahead, enough ahead so he can't look all the time. But she is, after all, naked and she does turn and this is when I see he doesn't look at it but could.

She turns often, sometimes to see where we are, sometimes to pick up her son. Her son—you can see by the grey under his black—runs a fever so he can't always walk. But he is big and can't always be held. She picks him up and walks, holding him. And she has this thing on her belly.

He doesn't look at it. He stares into the grass as he walks and he whistles. How can he whistle? I am too tired to whistle, and too hungry, but probably whistling is a good idea. It might spook something; it might keep that something away. Courage is what it sounds like, as if courage could be carried and whistled out, little by little.

The boy is named after him. Snotty-nosed and naked and greyly feverish, he hears me call his name and only he turns, the boy I want to pick up and hug but can't. We walk too far and have too far to walk. He walks now too and the name sinks into the high grass after he turns, after he turns and smiles, not like the whistling which only dips, and we go on.

If I whistle maybe I won't get what she has on her belly which is making it awfully hard to carry him. Whistling might mean courage—or more food. Maybe he has had more food somehow, or medicine. Maybe courage is a kind of preventive medicine he thought up. They don't whistle. I whistle. I don't care if he doesn't answer.

The thing on her belly is large and bulbous. They always say grapefruit or orange, some kind of fruit. Or watermelon. It does not mean pregnant, it is to one side, this fruit. He doesn't look at it although it is why we are walking.

The boy is not really named after him. The boy has this name because at his birth this white man sat by the fire. No one that color had come before, for the beer and to listen. He said his name and he listened. They liked the sound of his name, it was a little like one of their own. It was enough like their own that they took it. Not for him, but for its sound.

He didn't seem to take anything from them. He only listened and made movies of them. They didn't know how that could take something away because with film you don't see what the one who's filming is getting.

It is a kind of getting, the making of films, looking and not looking. You put up the camera and it looks while you look at the edge, the all-around-outside of the looking, to try to get everything, to get it all. At least that is how it is in documentaries. You see shapes and you try to get them and keep them inside the box.

This looking and not looking is why he doesn't see what is on her belly. Even with the camera, he doesn't see it. It is a habit, this way of seeing, and he looks at me the same sometimes. That is why I distrust him, but there are other reasons.

We walk. The boy falls. He picks him up, he carries him. What kind of pride does he think she has that he hasn't picked him up before?

I am caviling. I am nagging even in my head. We have been walking too long. Twenty miles in a morning, twenty miles before the sun is too hot, every day. You figure four miles per hour, walking, that's five hours, that's nothing. But it is something, believe me. Especially with so little food. Especially when we are supposed to be there already.

I must say I like the food. Maybe it's the hunger, maybe it's the faint division between dead and alive in the things we are eating. Maggots add protein, instant, no supplements necessary. And then there is boiled grain, as whole grain as it gets without eating the stalks too. Except for the cramps you have from eating it, the smell of boiling grain—so humid—really sends me.

This is what I think of, walking. There's also her thing on her belly and why I distrust him and the boy's fever, which must be worse since we haven't had water for awhile, but mostly I think of things to eat. This morning, getting that dead crust from my mouth, I tasted chocolate. By swallowing. The kind you buy in bumps that a machine makes thinking you don't want much at a time. That type has a wrapper flavor you can't get rid of, even if you melt it.

Chocolate would puddle here. I think of that, looking at her dark back, wondering why it doesn't sag with the weight of her little son and her belly and the heat and our effort. But he moves us on, he says, Don't you want this or that, either in English or in her language.

I understand some of her language. I mean the tourist stuff, the things you would need to say if there were any tourists here. That helps some in the trust department, which is different from the beginning when I didn't know any words at all and he did. I learned as quickly as I could without any dictionary or aptitude or cognates, those words that are part of the same family you speak usually, like chocolate and *chocolat*. This language is unwritten, it has only sounds run together, no nice stops in-between to make it easy to get the words one by one. Of course, all language is like that, coming out in a flood with only the breath making the limit. I learned by saying Charlie this and Charlie that, Charlie being what they use for What is. Having just the names of things is a little limiting because you miss how things are done and who is doing what with what and you get tired and fall asleep while he is talking.

He puts the boy down. He is checking our direction, turning and looking out at all the flatness. He has his hand over his eyes to see a little farther into the grey whiteness of distance here, and the heat waves. But it's not for direction really because how can he remember which way after eight years of not being here? It is she who tells him where we are, who reassures him, who picks up the boy and walks on. The one with the problem.

Is it death? Or is walking god-knows-where death with our little grain and little water? My head is so light and not connected to my moving legs and arms that I understand completely now the meaning of rhetorical, how a person could put out an important question and just let it float off. Not that I would say the question out loud, not with him swearing every other step how he will die soon, you just wait. Is this why he won't look at her, he thinks this thing on her belly is part of his death?

I want to hold that little boy and his fever and say his name like it is really him and I have him in my arms, dying. Only, of course, I would save him then to show him he is wrong. The little boy I want to hold because he is ill and has nothing, not even aspirin and he has to walk. I remember all the sore throats I had when I was small and white pillows and cold compresses and hot jello that didn't help much, and how he has none. But he is like an animal in his illness, not wanting to be touched or held, even by his mother. He wriggles down from her when he can, he wants to be in his body. Who blames him since the heat makes each of us so apart, the machine of our bodies running high in the outside temperature, especially his, so that everywhere something is touching is too hot. Even this old bottle I carry with its little water inside is too hot and the sweat between me and the glass makes it hard to hold. It slips and the muscles of my fingers ache, grabbing at it again and again.

But I say nothing.

■

Would I like a glass of cold water?

The idea of cold is so odd. Cold in a glass? Or even, water in a glass? You have to have something to compare it with, the very middle of the night when the body is next to the earth and not the fire, with the earth dark from your body on top of it—that is cold.

I say Yes, thank you.

She says, That will be a dollar. And leaves the room.

A dollar. A dollar for a glass of water? Even a cold glass of water?

When she comes back, bearing it, I say No, thank you, as polite as I think you should be with clergy.

For this is the wife of clergy. At least I think so since this is a mission and out the window I see a cross over what is said to be a clinic. But my tiredness makes it confusing—can you be a clergy doctor? As well as this asking for a dollar for a drink of water. Isn't charity part of the clergy position, or is there only the missionary position?

I laugh to myself and say, I changed my mind.

She puts the glass down on the table between us very carefully like it is a trophy and the sides of the glass weep with condensation. I look away from it because it is not polite to stare at something you've just refused but my hands sweat noticing the coolness, that is, the picture of coolness my brain makes to send notice. I look out the window or where the window would be if this matched the insides with its stereo, potted plants, tables and chairs, and out of the window hole and screen I see him walking with the clergyman.

Are you married long? she asks in the same cold water voice.

I want to say Yes, make the same kind of answer as with the water, because that will please her, that will answer her two questions at once—Long? and Are you?—making it easy not to be too specific. But seeing him walking outside next to the clergyman who could, if he wanted, marry us, I hesitate and the gap between her question and my hesitation grows into a No but a curious one. Not like the gap before the No to the water which could be impolite, and not No, we do not have a dollar, but No, you are mistaken, we are not married at all.

There they are, I say instead, and point at the air of the window hole to the woman and her grey child, the woman with the tumor on her belly. They are being moved from one line to the other by a man who drags along a rope with a knot in it, a knot that he likes to flick up into the air and land very near someone, even her when it takes her some time to move the boy and her belly to a new line.

I mean more by my There they are than just pointing

however, than just deflecting her from my by now obviously unmarried state unworthy of even the lukewarm glass of water now sweating between us, I mean that they are the ones we have walked days for, to get help, and why do you allow that man to treat them like that with his whip—or any of them?

She says Yes, there they are, and says, They clawed at the screen all last night, and she points to the window hole with its screen across it and, I think, bits of brown and black flesh stuck to it from the night before, not shadow. I look down and I see her hand move then toward the water in slow motion, so slow I see her hands are shaking.

She takes a drink.

They want to get in, she says, they want booma. You know what that means? To be strong, she says, not giving me a breath's worth of Means? Booma tet, she says, very strong. They want injections like others of their kind want drugs, they see someone get one smallpox scar and live and they want them all over. They think they will live forever with these injections. They want to live forever.

She drinks a lot of the water. I watch her. The condensation is gone from the glass so I can see just how much is left, just how much goes down. She doesn't finish it though, there is still about an inch of water left, cool enough, I think, when she tosses the rest into the plant in the pot next to her. Then she raises her shakey hands up to pat the hair on her head which is not coming apart like it is a hairdo but sits solid as the glass and shines an almost transparent white, the color of water, but a brittle white.

∎

In the dark it looks like a papaya. This is not a real dark but the dark from a barn that has no windows. And I'm not sure in this dark if I see what it looks like. I could be asleep. I should be, it is very hot, especially with no windows, and I walked so far today to get here—an extra ten miles—my legs throb. They quiver the way a deer we killed along the way did, for hours after. This quivering and the sound of my own language keeps my eyes open to the dark which is not sleep. I lie not that awake listening to the faint murmur of some language that must be mine, that could be mine as much as, anyway, the papaya hanging in the dark window above me, drying, could be mine.

He is outside, speaking it. He can talk all day in the sun, the heat heats him up and gives him energy, there are solar panels in his brain. Murmurs come through the cracks with the heat, they are talking together, about lunch because it is that time, in their language, in my language, to talk about lunch. Or they are talking between bites, eating and talking of lunch, sandwiches made out of ground grain, baked and ground instead of boiled, and he is not saving me any, he is not saving me a single bite. She is asleep, he is saying between bites, Let her sleep.

I could be, and these small pangs in my stomach are just leftover from eating the bullets of boiled grain, like buckshot, last night, and trying hard to digest them so many hours. Now I understand how a stomach can cause trouble, social unrest, real motivation with every eight or so hours of complaints, of suffering. But it is nothing compared to the lump on her belly, though I think lumps like that don't hurt until they squeeze hard into something on the inside, something important. I try to keep my pangs in proportion but they are mine and hers are hers and maybe a half mile away in the noon sun no one who lives here sits out in, like us in a snow storm, but because they have no place of their own and are just waiting and must wait where they are put, there she sits, and my small pangs wither, thinking of her in that sun with her belly and her son, feverish. Everyone gets out of the sun except this man who is with me.

The door jiggles. He steps inside and locks it behind him. The effect is a flash as if he appears from thin air, or light, in this case. He walks from his flash to the cot in the dark and touches the small of my back so I know he wants sex, he wants to put his hand down there inside my skirt and move it to my front.

Instead of food.

I wriggle and forget. I wriggle and forget and like it. I like the way he presses into me which is why I forget about trust and the question of food, and many other questions. But soon I find air which is no longer liquid between us but black and dry, hot and hungry. How can air be hungry? I feel it empty and open, so dark the sides are collapsed and he is suddenly breathing it in, sleeping like after a good lunch though I could not smell it, could not find crumbs. But he is clever and knows ways of keeping me going with sex so I won't find out, so my smell and taste do other things.

Or he could be as hungry as I am and sleeping, lightheaded, those curls in the dark nesting his paleness, his faint. I touch his hair and his hand moves out of the dark over the side of the cot and catches my hand and kisses the flat of it.

Will they take care of her? How much was the medicine? What about the little boy?

My hand touches the wrinkle of his mouth where I can feel just when the snore starts. He snores.

I reach up to the window that is blocked from the light. I want to do something that makes a difference, especially with hunger. I reach up to pull down the papaya, this low bulbed thing which looks wrinkled and dried but is surely sweet, I reach up to pull it down to share it with him, to give him some because he is hungry and has made love to me and kissed and is now so innocently asleep. I put my hand around its wrinkled black body and even pull as if it were tied up there by the wife of the clergy, away from rats, tied up to dry, and it shivers, shrugs me off with wings.

If I scream he will think I am afraid and then test me later in other places with that fear. No, I do not scream, I do not make one sound, not a single sound, and the feeling in my throat from that not-making is very much like the feeling I have walking with nothing to show for myself, no way to help. But no, I don't think that, I think feminist, it is not feminist to scream. And I drop the bat and it returns to its window with its own silence.

■

It's too much to say she tossed the rest of the cold water into the potted plant. She did drink some. How could she water the plants with one dollar water?

We are walking again. We are walking along a river that is broad and brown and famous. It is a relief to walk by a river, there could be a breeze from the river, a cool breeze.

There is no breeze, but you could go into the river to your knees and wipe the water over your neck and arms, the lukewarm water that cools finally, for an instant, as the air takes it. You do not go in farther than your knees because of the animals, mostly the ones that swim under the dark brown surface but some crouch, some have holes in the bank from which they watch, in case someone goes under or deep.

But we are walking and can't stop. To get from this or that dot on the horizon we must walk. Someday we will go along the river in a boat and have it push us but now it is going the wrong way. We are walking against it. But walking mile after mile is not bad. Every step is my own, I can walk from one end of the world to the other. I don't need a machine. I can walk and while the earth moves, I move. The tingling that rushes through my body from my bare feet to the back of my neck where the sweat pools is power. I keep going forward. How can I turn back? He wants to go forward. If I turn back I will be alone.

There are others who cross us, two moving black marks too small for buffalo, that most hated beast of these people, moving black marks too grounded for birds, even buzzards, black marks that are not the optical illusion of ostrich whose legs flower and disappear if you look too hard until they're just fluff on a stick, the stick moving. No, it is definitely someone, two someones, and he is slowing down like he wants to meet them. That is good for me who is falling behind, attracting birds.

■

Trust hasn't enough syllables. You want a word to wrap around you, with a lot of derivation, prefix and suffix, light, height, and weight, something that sticks. He is telling me about where he is from, its swamps and demons, its cement shoes of extra people, its plaster casts of footprints of creatures who shouldn't be there. He tells me about the blueberries we could pick just walking like this through a place with a house on it, he tells me about how the trees lean with the wind and grow small, he tells me how scallops dance just before they are taken. This last is in a joke, on the mating of scallops. This is instead of telling what he said to those two men that I didn't understand, the two men that are the size of insects when I look back but I do that only once because animals along this path hiss, have hissed, although he could have been what hissed. I am not sure.

The only other thing he doesn't say is how we paid for the woman and her son to stay at the mission. He doesn't say but I know my pack is lighter. I see a small crease where before it bulged out with items. I am not looking forward to the night, when I open it and pull out our things and try to sleep. I am sure it is the blanket that is missing, only a piece of a cotton sheet, not warm, but next to the earth at night when it is as cold as cold water, it was something. Now the missionary is selling this something again, not to her on the line, shivering—she has no money—but to someone.

I look over at the river. I would follow the river back. Then I hear the hissing and I walk faster, I walk that much farther.

We are seated under stars. We are seated on the thin white skin of a calf with the fur still on, the hair on the hide that is as stiff as my mother's Irish hair in black. But now almost white? The months are years here. I feel how long it takes for the light of these stars to arrive in such whiteness, in clusters which would be cruelly unfamiliar if I knew which were which at home or even noticed them there under all that electric light and movie light and TV glow that puts out most of the stars except for on the Fourth of July when people see them because they look up, and try to blow them out with fireworks.

Today is the Fourth. Of course I am not sure, one day I was sick and maybe I skipped a day and maybe not, maybe I put in two days since that kind of fever is a blackout and a stretch, a bulb burning out when you're not looking. But if it is the same day on this ball Earth, under these stars, it is right that there is a radio that plays this music that makes you want to lift your legs even if they have been lifted all day, music with words about how bombs flare at either sunset or rise—the small light of stars being at both ends of the sun's doings—and about flags.

People move in the dark against the radio and before the stars. They are what is so valiantly waving, in the thick smoke of the fire which is made from dry dung to keep bugs off, and the smoke of the pipes from a sharp strong leaf which, when burnt, isn't inhaled but held, but none of the smoke he sometimes makes out of the leaves from a suitcase that the people who are missing fingers and noses and even feet deal under the trees in bigger places. At least I don't think so. We have been walking all day and not stopping and the suitcase which he uses as a seat when we rest was not opened. But I don't know. He could have, in smoke this thick with this kind of music, with people here and not here.

Except not now. Now he is singing. He stands by a pile of dry dung waiting to burn and puts his arms out and moves his mouth and the words seem to come out of him, these words that some pop star in a gold stretch lowcut something according to the announcer is belting out in a high pitch to people in bleachers.

His lips move against what little light there is between the smoke and the stars and the fire, his hands beat on his chest at the same time as someone beats drums by the microphone of the radio. All across the camp wherever there are fires people watch, puffing and laughing, and the air over them is all white, staining the stars even whiter, a Milky Way on a Milky Way.

The fake singing is funny. It matches the marching that schlocks out, the floats described, the left-right leg lifts in nineteenth-century woolen uniforms through the heat of that place where they twirl guns for fun. Of course no one here but us, I think, understands the singing being made fake or even what the singing is to us coming out of this black box in this place so far from where the valiant waves are made so I am surprised when the man next to me flourishes his weapon, which is more a club than a gun it is so old-looking, with a broad flaring barrel the leg of a bell bottom would look good on, but maybe he is flourishing it to drive away bugs. It is not loaded, I think, because all his bullets lie drying on another skin, drying from being packed with black dust, drying right in front of the door of what we lean against.

It is while I am laughing at more of his fake singing that the gun goes off. It goes off far away so I look into the dark and stars, I look through the smoke past him who has stopped singing and is now marching in place, arm cocked, head back, and I see only smoke. No one gets up or heads for cover, whatever cover might be had here with land so plain and what we lean against basically land and twig. They know what?

He sits beside me again. He turns off the Fourth of July and doesn't say, About the shot? I think he knows as little as I do and Don't ask: a report from a car in the city, some big animal landing on dry wood from a height in the country? Then it sounds again, twice, and I turn faster the right way, knowing where, and see a man standing in the dark with two long boards he brought from a thousand miles north and from a thorn tree bare of all leaves behind him rise a hundred birds that have been squawking and fighting for roosts and who stop, settle in a second, goshawks, ibis, goatsuckers, flycatchers, shrikes and swifts and crows.

They are silent.

I say into the dark, You got me, in my own language which I am not supposed to be speaking, even to him. I say this because I didn't ask, Who's shooting?

I have to say something.

He begins to squawk. And others of those sitting with us squawk too until someone ends it with a kestrel's *shreeeee* that scares me.

■

In bed, that is, on the white calfskin with fur like my mother's soon-to-be-white-hair and with a mosquito net tented over me on sticks, a net with holes that admit only the more virulent, longer pokes of smaller bugs, me with a sheet—or is it his body?—wound like a shroud tight, our sheet already gone to pay for medicine, him so tight against me my breath works his and he stays awake, the flag of him being what I'm really wrapped in—in bed, I can't see the stars because we are inside what we lean against. Familiar or unfamiliar, I can't see them. But it doesn't matter—the light is so old anyway, hardly glinting off the gold lame singer whose words I now follow with a bouncing ball in my head. Each bounce makes tears come from how far away? and through how many long distance linkups we don't have? and against how many of those dead stars?

Sleeping on a skin is—very interesting, the way if you say that word interesting about a book you know no one would read it. Tossing on a skin is not turning. To turn you need give, and room. The ground under us is slick as linoleum when we are lucky enough to stay where someone has slept not long before us—no, slick as the stuff you lay in sheets so there's no seams at all, and as hard as a marble dais in another set-up and time, just right for a king to lie on in all his clothes, holding the hilt of his sword, and dead.

Nonetheless, I am willing to consider sleep on the skin. Anthems have played, there has been some sun, some walking under it, some of what I thought was gunshot. I pull at the sheet wound like a shroud—or is it him?—closer to me, as a shield, as a comfort, but my arm is extra, the one under me, it has to go up and out.

Rule one of sleeping: hyenas eat arms that stray out of nets. Even inside what we lean against? I ask. And I feel his head move up and down against my ribs and I hear the pack that harries a sheepbarn not far enough away, not nearly far enough away, and they do not laugh while they are doing it.

I make up jokes about the Fourth, about the man who

lives in the big white house with the many jeeps around it with their grin of guns, and the marchers around them with their own songs and flags that they wear around their middles instead of waving. I laugh instead of the hyenas.

■

When you brush your teeth you use ash. The fires from the dung glow with charcoal in the morning when there's ash, fresh ash. All you have to do is bend down and poke your finger into a little of it and rub your finger clear to your gums and spit, and again, and then your teeth are white. The blackness of the ash and its lye work better than paste with sugar in it. In the end nothing is dirty, not even your finger after you suck it clean or spit all around it but you can use a twig if you want, a twig from a tree that is quickly brush when you push it against your teeth with ash. This twig gets dark with the ash in its brush and when you have made all the teeth white, you put it back in the ash where it catches and flares under your spit, then burns. The rest is the same.

I know this. I go to the river as soon as I can't pretend the dark around my lids is still dark, and I take with me my brush and its faint green smear of paste, whatever I have left.

The back of the handle of the brush says New York if you look at the ridges of plastic where you hold it in too much light. I only notice this when I set it down on a clod of upturned clay which is frozen in dryness to rock shape, in the light that comes then, off the river where you go if you are not in a big hurry to do what people in the morning must do first and here do for fish. While I am doing this, I see the embossing, practically a note in a bottle, a letter from home, two letters to be exact, an N and a Y. I see them sharply because the brush rolls on its back on this clod and an ant plies for the letters in a line for the sweetness that lies at the end of the brush, and then two ants, until there is an arrow of ants, pointing.

I thank the ants for showing me the marks.

After using two sheets of paper that we can't write on because it is too thin, using all the corners, every fold, all he allows because he is the one who has been here before and knows how much, I drop the paper into the soup of this famous river, a dark and mineral soup, and the paper rushes off. Then I wash myself with sand and then with a piece of soap that I stroke on, a sliver's worth because more is just suds, then I pick up the brush and bring it to my face and I use it.

The water takes what foam I make fast, pushing up to the New York, pushing over. Just another place, I say, but with the same moon. Forget the stars. Then I look around to see the morning moon but it is gone, just a little foam on the edge of the horizon, pushed off by this sun that isn't mine, huge and gory with its edges solid and cutting.

The water glitters with sun so I look away and see my hand which is next to the water and this is when I notice the brush is not there, the whole brush is gone. It is not that I let it go. It is that the water has taken it and will keep it.

I put my hand to my forehead against the brightness that is already pulsing, and squint my eyes downriver. There the river is still dark against that white sun. The water here moves like a person against my legs, in a rush, at the same temperature as me, in the same hurry. I move my hand from its shading and put it in the water as if I could catch my brush from a person who has so long ago left in such a hurry.

I hold up my hand. Where the brush should be is still air.

Better than nothing, I almost take that as.

Better than ash.

I walk back. It is a long way because no one wants anyone to see that he is doing this every morning like everyone else. Except the children who are doing it closer. because of dysentery. So I have a long way to feel my clean teeth, to look over the piles of glowing ash that I pick between and have to look forward to.

■

He is peering into me with a flashlight. No one's there, he says and shuts it off. But I wish.

I make a sound that says Great! the way you would if your legs were pressed apart and someone were leaning between them, wishing for something you didn't want.

No one can see us, right? I roll sideways against the net that is tucked into the white skin on the ground, so I will be in the way of someone seeing my legs spread through the cracks of the basket that covers the hole to the outside.

He puts the light into his mouth so his cheeks glow the color of his blood, so I can see teeth, and breathes loudly. My teeth see you, he mouths around the light.

I giggle.

I pull the light away from him but not without him first

sucking at a breast that comes too near. I take the light and flick it into his eyes where he is sucking, over my heart. You are under my command, I say. Confess. The truth.

He goes to his haunches, his penis between us. Always invoking the truth when it's god you want. What's on the penny? God's the one to trust.

I didn't say trust. I said truth.

You know the movie where they're driving the dynamite over some European border—not Boris Karloff but the other creep with the high voice? He says Trust me.

He makes his voice high, he's between my breasts again.

The light that has rolled to what we lean against now dims.

I can fix it, he says, sitting up again and maybe he means the light or maybe he means me because he's soon down again.

A bat at the top of what we're sheltered under gets a bug while I shift, while I look for a place that isn't right up against the net where the bugs and now a bat are moving.

He is humming when he comes into me, humming that song from the Fourth. Before he mouthed the words, now he doesn't move his mouth.

With one hand I reach into the dark outside the net. I grope and find my pills and nothing else, no snake. I pop a pill out with one hand and suck on it and its faint sweetness, what sugar is like through paper, I hold it under my tongue. But I'm laughing when he makes it on the verse with all the exploding, then feeling for the plastic bubbles, which are full and which are empty, counting how many days when.

Could I have the light?

It's gone, he says. He moves the switch and it is still dim in the high part where the bat is.

I finger the holes, putting one heat in order with the next. When I look up, still adding and remembering, a moon comes through where a snake could, where someone could see.

■

There is no reason to worry. Everything is under a kind of control. Besides, you can buy worry here, in packets that you hang with other packets on bare trees until the wind comes and takes them. Or you strap the packet to the top part of your arm under your shirt like some Jew with his packet. If you have a shirt. I do because all I am is some pretend black person, with worry. I pretend because no one is white here and I do not want to be no one. The one who makes me someone in my color is gone for a while. What while?

Today will be better. Or perhaps Today will be. That is how I read the smoke rising from the camp in air that must be cool but not for far. The rippling that the smoke makes stops above the woven spires of where we stay, except when a hawk or one of the vultures flap through. Then the ripple shoots up a little further, follows the bird or pushes it.

Better or not, here it comes. The sun rises on this smoke, rises until it is someone else's sun, not mine. If it ever could be mine, something this huge. Maybe his. He thinks big but he's not. He gets height in curls and the way he speaks, always good with the words in how he hears others talk. I see him now pick his way through the boys bending over the smoke of the fires, cut out dark the same against the sun as he bends to blow the ash from the kernels they're offering hot off the dung or to take toothpaste from. He's all black.

There's nothing I can do about that, except move and see him different. That is the hardest part, moving. That cool before the sun will ripple away if I move, ripple up. Let him come to me.

He doesn't. The full-sized sun rises in its whiteness and movement stops, all movement stops. Birds still find currents far, far up and I can hear a snake move against the high part of where we sleep but I too lean back with my belly that moves even if I don't, in and out, tighter and tighter, against whatever happens in hunger. I lean back as the day starts, expecting nothing or less—heartbeats, a turn of a hand as a change of landscape, worry.

This worry is not at all as big as his. He talks in his sleep about what will bite him or who will shoot him and I don't think it's about pointing the camera either. Not with that kind of worry, the groan-in-the-sleep kind.

Money we don't have so that's not his worry either. It's mine but I am not groaning much, at least not to wake him or attract the hyenas like he does. We gave our money to someone to keep, what you do here. Or you wad it up in a cloth and tie it with string you braid from trees and leaves and hook it on a piece of wood that helps hold up the place where you stay. But we don't stay long anywhere so he gives it to someone to keep, somewhere else. Anyway we don't need much because what could we spend it on? Cold water? If I want eggs and we have no grain to give for them, they want cassettes, as I find out.

And it is not to open them and string the tape around the bare thorn tree to pretend a Christmas, although that can happen. And it is not to wear the tape under the arm in a tight packet of worry either, although that can happen. I once saw this. They want cassettes to have their songs in one place so they can play them while the singer is gone, they can listen and sing back and look at each other—and not the looking into non-place like we do, listening.

What I write is all those words they say in song on cassette. I move under this sun only to move my pencil across a page on my knees. I write these songs first in their language by breaking out the words that heave from them in a river as long as the famous one theirs feeds into, and then I make them mine. I move them to match the way I think, and the way I like them to stand next to each other, picture to picture or sound to sound. I hear words in voices around me, from one person to the other but they seal me in, they don't say We see you or Come to us but This or That to each other. Only he says or doesn't say and he has left. I write to hear something since he is not here. I put their words on paper instead of hearing the words return to their river and disappear.

But I do not have their words on these papers long. I write and my sweat drags after my writing, erasing it, and ants follow that eat lead. I know this is true because on the last page the writing is gone but a lace is left.

I walk to the tree. This is some distance because all the trees close-by are burnt or used to build. The tree I find is bare of leaves and thorns and bark, with only packets of worry hanging from it, packets of skin from cats or cows that have dirt or twigs or spit inside, that hang the way we would put globes of glass on trees. I stay there, not moving but writing, the place where I walked from now a small point of black against the brightness.

We give them cassettes instead of money, blank ones, ones that don't already have songs on them that I ask for. They won't sing slow enough for me to write the words so I have them sing to the tape so I can play it over and over in a way they don't like. They like to play the whole song from start to end but I crawl along with Charlie this and Charlie that. Since one tape is a lot of words to Charlie, I have extras, I have blanks. But not for long. There are many songs and few eggs and I get hungry, eating only once a day.

When to eat if it is only once? You guess First thing, a good breakfast makes a good scholar, the right start, a punch in the gut. But no, that does not do. When the sun goes down and the snake relaxes and things wack around all night just outside your net, not to mention the loud noise in your gut, you can't sleep if you don't eat. Eat at night. Once then and you won't wake up in the dark because your gut hurts. You won't waste sleep.

Starving is another thing. With starving I remember from reading you get sleepy. But eating a big bowl of sour sorghum under an inch of rancid butter, dipping your clamshell down below all that clear yellow slick and bringing the sorghum through it, steaming in couscous formation, in amongst all the other clamshells spooning, is not starving, even if it is only once a day.

So when I see him hand the two girls my tape I am not

so upset, I don't think there goes one of my blanks. I think eggs in the nighttime after couscous, what a good idea. But after I finger the shell from the thin white skin that holds it onto the boiled part, a kind of sack that the eggs sits in that you wouldn't even notice if you were not treasuring every morsel and its wrapping, after I finger the shell, sniff it for any delicious hardboiled eggness, I remember it was a tape with songs—or something. It had something on it. I know this because I count the boxes, because the boxes are like money, and this one had a mark on the front and the wrapper off and because none of them now have their wrappers off, a cellophane that goes all around it, not a stuff that easily goes from off to on.

This is what I worry about out here but I go on writing. I write until someone comes—larger, slowly larger against the brightness—and asks, Why do I go away from them, am I sick? until I understand.

I am sick, I say, and touch my forehead which, as a child I meant, I'm pretending.

That someone sits down in the sun because I am sick and waits and talks though I don't know what about. I know words in the flow but by the time I make them into my language the flow is past. I smile, I nod. Do I look more sick if I smile and nod? I want someone to talk while the ants are working on my paper, taking my words, and her voice comes all around me, making the words move by themselves, like talk in my language, only not. I like it.

She talks and I wish I had a cassette and the machine to get her words down. But I am not the only one who uses the machine and the cassettes. He uses it sometimes to record off the radio not only the anthem but songs like

"Louie Louie" and crooner tunes like Cat Stevens who ought to be Sinatra, whatever the station is that gives Easy Listening which is about right for here with the sun on for so long. Everyone looks away or walks off when he plays it outside, or worse, looks at us, so usually it is at night when we play it, inside where we can crouch down and smile and sometimes stand and turn once, depending on how big the inside, how big the ones who lent the place are, in status. Unless it's a holiday.

Is that him coming over this flatness back to here? There is no food to mark his coming, no food between when he is black before the sun and when the moon is coming to blacken him in his white skin. If it isn't him and he doesn't come back, will there be food for me who is only a woman and just white, someone fearing the sun, its everyday up? And who has not been here before? I listen to her talk to become her, to eat.

■

We are dancing in the small space inside, two steps around and two shakes, a turn in the night and a catch, and I say to him, Did you get the eggs with one of my cassettes?

He says, Stop. You think I stole one from you?

I dip and bow and am not caught with his arm. The music is going on and he is standing an elbow away from me but he is not moving, he is not catching.

Both of us are black in this space.

None of mine are gone, I say. I just wondered. About this music, if you gave some away.

He takes the cassette out of the machine and holds it up. We still have some music.

Good, I say. Good.

What do you think I did? he says.

I just asked about the other cassette, the one you gave for eggs.

Ask away, he says. You'll be sorry, he says. Then he leaves.

I turn this way and that in the little space.

On a trip like this there is always surprise. Even not moving is a surprise, even not making this new film of his, day after day. Most of the time we do not mind the surprise, it's why you take a trip, but sometimes we do, like surprise to do with the few things we have, so we split things up, not to lose them. I have the passports, he has the things we use for money.

I turn this way and that. I am not used to no money, even if it is just a bag tied way up over my head somewhere else, even if it is a cassette. I like to think I can touch it. And that eggs will be mine when I am hungry.

Why does he worry about me worrying about the cassette?

I worry. But I have two eggs.

■

These hillocks rhyme with bullocks and that is what they remind me of, these cows here that move along, leg, leg, hump, against the real flatness that is the landscape but also they remind me of the plains where I come from that have just a percentage of this horizon, but enough. Especially with clouds piled at every edge, especially with the smell of rain in a wind blowing from so far away it could be from where I come from, that smell of something that has no chance of falling.

The man who walks in front of me wears a map on his back of the way we are going, that is, the hummock and plains all pricked out in some design of scar across his back. On his front where his face starts, just over the brows, six straight scars run like that's where you Tear Here to get inside, scars to the bone that show he's as tough as a woman who gives birth. It's a map of where he's been, not of where we're going. At least not me. It's for men only. The man I am with has only this hole in his lip good to wiggle screws through. Even he draws a line (does not cut it) at this bone-deep slicing, the way I do at birth. I don't even think about birth but keep my eyes on the rise and fall of that man's shoulders and the map as he walks. He is in front and I follow, always in single file so talking is hard but the map is good.

He sings while he walks, with our things on his head, he sings around what teeth he has, the ones they didn't pull out with the point of a spear when he was as small as the fevered boy. He says when we start that I should not look like one of those animals that bother the sheep in the night, I should have these teeth out like his. He says he has a spear, he can get them out the same way his came out. He means that we look funny with our side teeth in, those you tear with if you are part dog. I can't say Orthodontia, see where mine were taken to make me look the way we think we like to look so I think he is singing about how I should change my teeth.

He likes me. He does not laugh at how I speak my few words, not like he does.

It is a long time later that we come to a river that is not the famous one we usually follow but another one that runs in the way. It is deep, you can see by the muscles the water makes going along, as if the water were walking in front of me with its hillocks and plains.

We stand on the bank with the man with the map on his back and he smokes a cigarette which is made of a page of the book that I carry, and some long dry leaves. The book is *Chrome Yellow* or *Tristram Shandy*, anyway a thick one I thought I would read all of and haven't and won't now, at least not while this man wants to smoke it. But it is a kind of money, and it is mine.

He smokes my page and we sit until he wants to smoke more and then I find another not-so-good part and more leaves.

I could use the rest of the book to find my way back.

He is rolling his cigarette, wadding and crushing the leaves into the middle of the page, when he says *nyang* and points to the river.

The river in front of us matches the famous one in color and content, less the toothbrush I'm always sure I see, with the same shadows of birds overhead watching for fish that add to the darkness of the soup here and there so I cannot tell myself if something is in it but there could be.

Like crocodile.

And he, the man who is not smoking, his face is shaking

the way it does when he dreams, and he says, Not by land but by water, and he looks down into it.

This is not meant for me since it is so mumbly, so I pretend not to hear. Where are they? I ask. There's not a floating log in sight.

They sleep in underwater caves, he says with his face still shaking. Don't you remember? That's where they take you. It's not chomp, chomp, chomp. More like drag and drown.

He is the one who has been here before, he knows where we can walk. Just not here exactly. Here there are no maps but this man's back. Only he knows which way.

I could turn back now. I could leave him here with his shaking, with his by land or by water.

He tells me, twitching, he heard once about a man who was trying to get people to build a new kind of boat, one that would move better on this river, and he went for a swim to show them if it flipped there would be no problem. But he drowned. Somewhere around here. But with help, he says. They found a watch in the animal's belly, still ticking.

I could leave. But now I am part of a story. I am standing on a riverbank deciding on death or no death. He is the one who is shaking, the one with only a dream. He says, When god wants you he will take you.

He has some belief in god. He says this is what people say here and the guide says Yes, when he says it in his language. Yes, and shrugs.

I can walk if he can't.

Which should it be, I say, the fox or the cabbage?

I am trying to lighten up.

The man is already holding our camera, our clothes, the

long leaves and the suitcase. I hold up the bottle of water and my pack and I follow. I hear him come along, and his breathing that is rough, that is nervous.

The water shoves around me in different places all the time so when the bottle is easy to hold up, it suddenly isn't. And plenty feels like something: the bottom and its half-buried branches, the pieces of leaves just under the surface, the sweat joining the place where the water rises on my shirt.

But we are then there and no one is under, and all are whole. And when I turn, entirely out of the shallows, every bit of the river running off me, I see the water just as dark and deep as before and nothing in it.

And I see he is not shaking in front of it except to get the wet off, and the man is the same, asking for a new cigarette with a little rolling of his fingers.

If the matches are wet, he says with verbs and with motion, Not to care. He has his hands, he has two sticks.

I tear the page slowly.

This is the swamp: noise. This is the largest swamp in the world and the fish after the bugs and the fish eagles after their fish and the swatters and the crocs reveling in what must have been a very quiet place at the beginning with one-cells oozing in half in rhythm is all noise.

I hear him anyway under it: he whispers to someone in their language, and one word sounds like oil but what does that mean, an open *o* or different, a sound with a *u* that is a kind of comb? I think. Or the open *o* and *l* which means they are in a special part of speech—are in, and can be attached to past tense to mean Are way in.

We are way in. We are so far in this swamp they speak different. But he could be saying oil. He is the one I am traveling with, and in this language I once heard radio for the box we listen to. A cognate! He is speaking while that box is playing softly outside, and I am in a dry spot behind a net, not too far away. He is speaking low however, and the swamp is high.

I don't lean out of the net to hear better. I am happy here. Nets in a swamp are required. In the boat that we took to get here, nets went all the way around everywhere but behind them stood too many people. When the people all moved to one side to see an animal in the water, the net on that side touched the water sideways. Besides letting water in in quantity, the net kept me in, and I felt grid on my cheek and its strength, the net blocking me from safety. I put my foot on it and tried to tear it and couldn't, then people or the animal and then the people shifted so the water inside was just a mix of fear-pee and leak. And silence. Except for the bugs outside and the people who were inhaling for shrieking.

Now there is so much noise I can't tell what kind of oil he is speaking of, are in, or oil, or a comb. I am interested because any word I might already know that they know is one more, one less for me to learn. When he comes in, I ask.

That is, when he crawls in through the low door flap on his hands and knees and swears because bugs follow him, I ask.

Okay, he says, this is what it means: a word at the end of some words to make an impression. Like, say, ummmmm. I write that down.

All the bugs are excited by his coming in and get under the net when he raises it. He takes off his clothes anyway. While they get at him and he turns and turns and they get me too, I say nothing. He offers to cut an *x* into each bite and suck the poison out. This is so kind, considering all the sucking. I hug him. I want to know more, I say. I need to.

Listen, he says, that's all you can do. Remember the rules, he says next, as he leaks from me, his dark body in sleep smoothing out amid so many clucks and coos, flops and swoops all around, he says, You'll be all right with the rules.

■

She eats and I record her. I am pointing the machine at her because the wind comes between us when I point it away. Because of the wind I have a fence of cornstalk woven tight between my machine and her. Her eating is what I record, not so much the man singing beside me. But I don't know this from all the singing he is making at such a level and all the others who are shouting at him while he sings because the man is so good. Until her teeth break through the fence and almost touch my machine, until her tongue swipes at the controls.

This means Give up. I fold the cord of the machine into itself, not the cord with the plug because who would have one here but the one that leads to the mike, when a woman who has been listening and shouting says, Come with me. She says this before the cord is gone.

I know these words. Come with me. I put in some hope that sometime someone would say them with me in mind but had never heard them that way. Usually Eat! or Here! with just as few syllables as children get. Now, with this Come with me, I come.

She hits the cow with the flat of her hand away from my machine because she, the cow, now likes the feel of tape on her teeth or so it seems, as she can't get enough lick from the plastic cover, a coating which is all that keeps her from the real candy.

Swamp cows.

I walk with the woman to a place and leave him behind. He is not shooting film anyway. He sits with the men getting color. This means he talks and they talk and after a while someone sends for beer, which is when the color starts. He is helping me since men come to sing before and after color and I am too shy to stick a mike into the face of one of these men with just as few clothes on as the man with the swamp on his back, in fact, less. So less that no clothes is accurate, even if it is a swamp and bugs bug us. Clothes don't help here really, and catching a bug in the folds and re-stinging is possible. Stinging through is possible. This is a way of describing the no clothes that avoids the folds of organs down in front, but they are not what keeps me from getting songs myself because they are so many I don't notice fronts after a while. But the overall size of the men I notice, especially with the unbroken length. The size compares with the tallest of men, very closely.

They are sometimes a foot taller than I am and I am not short. They are too tall.

I walk with the woman and leave them behind. Other women come with us, put down their stones, pick up their children and follow. We make a place for everyone, then the woman who took me takes a mat that is a door and stuffs it in place. Another woman gives me a calf skin, banging it so hard against her fist dirt jumps off. She says Sit and I sit. The other women too, they take their places, if not their skins, all around me.

I smile. I do this as much as I can when I don't know what I am supposed to do or when people are speaking at each other around me and I think it is about me. This kind of smiling needs good muscles, as much as the man with the map on his back needs his in his legs when he walks or this woman in front of me whose finger taps at the end of a long pipe and I see how the shoulder works the finger, all the way to the bands across the chest that keep the breasts up. I am doing push-ups with those muscles in my face when I pull the cord out of my machine and turn it on even if there is no song for them.

But there is. They sing. One at a time a woman comes up and I put her name first and then whatever of her life she has made into song goes on, sometimes for a long while.

We listen.

By the time a knock breaks in, the women and me are rapt, me because I hear more words, I know some of the way the songs are going but I am more like a windshield with dead bugs collecting words that I hit, than living in the song with meaning. But it makes me not want to breathe in case breathing makes a difference in understanding, so when the knock comes, it breaks in.

Now a knock needs wood. There is not even a thud on daub and wattle. The man sticks his head in the hole that the basket was over and beats on some round old vegetable that must have seeds inside, and hard ones. He knocks on this and three times says I have to go because they are ready, three times so I can understand.

I understand even that they have made a new windscreen to replace the one that the cow ate, but barely. It gets noisy, as noisy as swamp noise. First the woman who has been singing to my machine and to her friends, screeches in a pitch unknown to me but maybe to birds here. Then two women stand and swipe at his ears with the switches they carry for bugs. This is while the other women laugh and call out things like, He is a fish. I think.

He does not stay past his third time telling me. His face shows he expects a woman of my color and small size to obey him but I do not. He says the name of the man who is not shooting but talking to get color several times in parting so I do not forget who else needs to see me do this.

I smile. That man who is out there with the color will not speak to me for some time because the other men will see he cannot make me do what he wants so he will lose face which means he cannot do any shooting for a while. A lost face cannot shoot, even if it was going to. But I can feel the smile on my face be less work as I switch on my machine, as I call to the next one a few of my simple words and she comes and sings.

■

Petty and not petit, he says. Tit, he says, getting one half of mine in his hand, for tat. So domestic, your leaving me for the women.

I groan, caught. Why not domestic?

He reviews: In this swamp, this is a place that should see a different drama, not just be backdrop, with people with no names who get in or out of the way, and foliage that needs a lot of words to let you see what it isn't. It should not be just love story.

I see, I say, some swamp thing is needed.

Be part of the place, he says.

He's kissing me against the swamp bank, half sunk in swamp. We are out to see a deer that can walk on swamp because the deer is so light, but it is so shy we must hold very still and stay quiet. So he is kissing and whispering and fondling.

Marry me, he says almost without breathing, with so much kissing.

Because I'm domestic? I say but I have a Never ready, a Never with a laugh that says my surprise.

He doesn't let me. Petty isn't pretty, he says. He kisses me. He says, If it's not nice, say it backwards three times for a divorce, like Arabs.

I kiss back the Me Marry part but why do I want it and not want it, with a Never and without? With trust like a swamp?

Okay, he says. No love story. Adventure?

An old married couple, I say, live in a swamp.

He holds his breath and sinks slowly, fingers pinching nose, the swamp so slowly licking up him I think for a bit it's sucking.

But I don't save him. He eyes me when he's chin high in it. Suck, suck, suck, he says and reaches for my chest, my breast to pull himself out.

Wife, he whispers, take thy monster.

I say, No, but I stick out my hand and I lift, I lift anyway.

Boys come from the long grass to watch. They carry spears twice the size of themselves for fighting with each other and prodding the cows, the cows that must be walking on a drier place than this, but the spears are down so they can watch. The boys must be here to watch us or the animal we are waiting for. But in their coming they flush the animal so quickly it is only small and nothing more, just color, and they don't even raise their spears so that is not the why they are here. It must be us.

He stops kissing and proposing.

The boys keep coming, they pick up my glasses which I have left on the swamp hyacinth, a kind of pest whose green grows in thick beds all across the water and block it, then grows right up the side of the bank and further, they try my glasses on there, one at a time, with a kind of mime, seeing through them, the voyeur's mime. Or it seems to me mime, since I can't understand what they're saying or see how they look at us without my glasses. I want to jump up and shout No but he shakes his head at me. You left them out, he says. Now, don't scare or bother them.

They are my only pair of glasses but I keep my tongue and say I'm sorry about the women and their songs if it keeps us from beginning the film.

Don't be sorry, you will need songs.

He wins.

I say, Don't you think a sun like this makes people different?

The boys go still as flamingos, standing one leg up on the knee of the other. This is the way the boys rest instead of arm to hip and slouch. But it doesn't look like resting, it looks like listening.

A sun like this has to make people backdrop, I say. Remember how that woman and her son looked sitting in it when we left them?

He has that I'm smoking a cigarette look, without one. He does not look at me but at the grass.

The boys leave my glasses, drop them on the soft swamp hyacinth, and start to creep. One giggles and slaps bugs, one spits.

I lunge for where the glasses have gone but he stops me, shakes his head. Wait, he says, wait.

I sit back.

I can't even eat right, I say. Men want me for my color to eat with them so other men can see how great they are to have such a person with such skin with them, and female. I'm just in the way of women if I eat with them.

I'll give you a club to keep dogs off children who are eating. A real job, he says without looking at me, looking into some distance I don't see.

I'm angry now, at the real job part, I turn away, I'm smoking.

Let me film how your breasts rise out of the water, the nipples like bubbles, he says, and looks at me as if I am not dressed and as wet as he is where he is putting his swamp hands on me.

I am not happy enough to say Yes but the idea of the film

is good, getting it to go through the camera, that's good, that brings me closer to getting out.

I am thinking what matters, the getting out after all this time, or the film, or what I am doing with their language, when too much noise happens right near us. The boys come together, their voices rise from the rushes from whisper to shrill, to crow, and they raise a very long snake from the ooze at our feet and drape it over their shoulders, six boys' shoulders with the spears still sticking in the snake, with the snake writhing six boys' length.

It's not us, I say. We are backdrop.

He smiles up at the one cloud of the day and stands on one foot and leg as if shaking off pee. Mud slides from it. He lifts the other out of the swamp and walks away.

I stick my hand under my skirt and welt some of the cloth over my fist and fingers. I flex my fingers into an *o* with the welt on top and close the skirt part over a chunk of clay.

They—a boy with a mud cow and some sores, the two girls with miniature water pots, both with iron around their wrists and waists that is make spiked to hurt anybody who comes too near, and their mother or sister or someone who is holding up a heavy log by its middle aiming but not yet pounding it up and down into the corn at the bottom of the hollowed-out log—they laugh.

No wonder. I am already in reverse face here, that is white-face, already in clothes with no purpose in this place and hence ludicrous, and already mute trying to speak their language, and already extra. I don't need big feet or face paint.

Even if it is just children, I want to make them laugh because of my clowning and not the rest, myself. It is charm, the way, in my place in the world, my head goes to one side listening, even if I am not, and why I smile and nod and try for something funny in the words I make. Here, if I can't make those few words right, I make them funny.

They laugh.

But I have too few words: crocodile and my bad ways of saying eat and run and barn. They almost go. But I find if I make those words into a shriek, they mean more than just the saying. And if I repeat the word with just a slight shift in shriek, this they like too, again and again.

Unless it is me they laugh at, and not my shriek. I look at them: their faces split and even the woman's, who now spits on my head to show more of her pleasure, and I go for more success, I try the story of beating up, using two clumps of clay, and no rolling pin, just a crocodile, and a bird in the welts of cloth over my fist. I make the crocodile sound which is what? and tweet and pound the clay into dirt. All the while I talk my words until they run out and I am left with car, hat, remember.

Charlie this, I must say. Charlie that.

The boys and the girls go into chorus to tell me. The woman pounds. I Charlie close to her, until I can almost touch the log, until if she misses I will be under it.

She shows that she sees me by stopping, by wiping the sweat off her head onto her hand and the back of her skirt. She looks as if I should say, Could I give you a hand? but I can't say that so I take the log, that is, I stretch my own two hands around its wideness and lift it.

As a cylinder, almost not a log, it is heavy. It has no bark I could use to grip it. I grip anyway, I lift it with more force than I think I have and I drop it, I drop it in.

The mortar, the bigger cylinder which is hollow, shakes and maybe I crush a kernel of corn and maybe I don't but the woman is standing back, she is watching, and the children are running to get more to watch. I smile, the one with many muscles that tie up both cheeks, and I hand her back the pestle. No.

The woman wants me to do it again. She makes her hands move the way mine did, she is laughing.

I could stop and make the smile that shows I don't mind. This is something I can do. I could stop and run into the place where we have put our things and stay there polishing lenses or sweating on a page in the dark of it.

Until she comes to get me and repeats what she wants me to do.

I could not understand.

I stand there. What is the difference between my making the fun and having the fun made of me? In the end, and whose end? The ones laughing or the one making them laugh? I like the sound of this laugh and the way I am someone, not no one, when I pound.

I pound. The lifting is not as hard as the dropping. The pestle shifts when you lift, when you aim down with the heaviness that right away starts to slip it wants to go down so much. I almost miss twice and the birds—small ones, confetti in their fluttering yellow and red and sudden coming—rise with a spring in their stick legs and thin wings and settle twice. They want me to miss.

I do not. I think of the food I will get in the night and how much less if this falls and the birds feast. I aim and aim.

The woman is now two women and four children, then more. One of the women starts a song for me, high and to rhythm—what rhythm I make. They clap along, all of them. I mumble like I can follow the words, like I know them, so I don't have to watch them watching, me mumbling so I can do Punch and Judy with the grain and still have some dinner.

Soon I can't stop. I sweat and I try to stop but they clap more, they sing more. I keep going. Every time in my life I have this moment of knowing to stop and not stopping, there is a surge of Yes, there is something. This time I am part of them, I am not no one.

I am a machine inside their machine. I go up and plunge this log in, I go up and down. I have seen these machines going up and down, those that go deep into land, pulling and sucking the hot slick black up. But here corn gets broken and floured with my up and down, the log slips in my hand's sweat, gaining more weight each time I grab and plunge. Still I think, Charlie oil? Why haven't I asked before? I don't want to know? I want to keep oil with the other few words that are mine? I want to watch each of the women, one at a time, each with her half-teeth and ornaments and different face as I ask, as she answers Oil?

But I drop the log wrong. In thinking this, I miss and the grain goes to the birds who have been watching better. The women whirr at the birds, they whirr in mock flight, or fight, punching the air but while they laugh. It is the laugh they have been waiting to make, a held-in one that would fill a room if that's where we stood, fill it and then overflow it with echo.

I press my hands into my skirt, the hands that have sweat on both sides, then I scoop at the grain. I beat at the birds. I put a smile to my face and it smiles.

Look at this flour. I sift my hands through the white that has fallen, that the birds swoop for. I made flour.

■

Hot is what you feel here, and dirty. The glow off the ground which is brown in the light is just about gold and that is almost imagined, how gold on a face or a tree or just in the air, hanging, can be. Pictures in magazines show this gold on women with breasts out, and it is a trick is what you think, the camera is there and some flash is here. But the air draws us into its gold until any other is not to be imagined. You can't imagine that gold elsewhere, or an elsewhere without it. Then your arm is in it, turning and gold, and if it weren't for the hot and the dirt you would not believe it.

The degrees of heat and its light turn lumps of grey precious, turn faces over pots, their sweat drops, into gold, but the dark is just hot. Especially the dark inside, without windows. The heat creeps in without the gold, through the stalks of what is woven all around—no, heat can't creep, it is always there, from before the insides are made, before the eye has its inside. The heat heaves and a glue just as early attaches itself to dirt, the kind of glue that sticks cells together gets at the dirt, then skin. The dirt rides the heat onto the skin and sticks. If you were to join with someone, balls of it and peeled skin would pile up in a slick between you and the heat you were making with that someone.

That is, mud.

This is not to say I lay with him, making this mud. He lies in the dark without me, counting spiders. I am not sure about the spiders. When I move to the door where he is, he says, Spiders, and when I say, Let me help you, he says, Don't talk, I'm losing track.

Someone else is there with him. I don't know who since there are no windows and I have not been here always, in the gold light, but have walked to the river before the light got gold.

Why are there no windows? I ask a man who is sitting also, who has been sitting so long we have made some talk.

He says if you have a lover the husband can throw a spear at you through the window.

This he says slowly and with many over agains and my Charlie this? as well as his hand pointing and himself running to the outside with a pretend motion of the spear and the death scene after, not to mention the one in which the woman and the man are making love.

It is not funny. What is funny is the people where I come from and their stories of armor at the same time as the windows they thought up, all that armor and stained glass pretending it is not for the husband.

What is not funny are the spiders. He is inside seeing all these spider legs move and not having me help him. Or is he lying with this someone inside whom I hear in thuds so silent they just raise the heat a small bit, a degree? I am not afraid of spiders, which he knows—but how many? Too many of anything, legs, people, makes fear happen. That is why he's counting. For me.

To keep me from fear?

The man who sits beside me and knows about windows thinks I am a nurse and can what? For what? He is healthy. I can see all of him and even where the insides might show on the outside—around the face—he is well. But the end of his forearm up to the very top of his shoulder bubbles with scars, a scar I know and that is not known now where I come from: smallpox. What the missionary said is true: it is from his pointing at these bubbles that I know he wants me to make more of them, that women of my color in this light do this.

He bends his arm to show me why, to show me his arm's strength, how his arm has power from these bubbles.

No one I know has this problem of disease that kills you and your friends in a day so I don't know why exactly he wants more except as magic. And except for the moment in a room with someone in white who says, Look at this on a paper, and See this, I would say magic too. Make a hole in the arm and hurt and a bubble and you won't die. Well, make me two of those.

He has twenty.

But I don't have the one more he wants. This he doesn't believe, he says I have one inside. He won't take No. He's heard No before. After a while, No turns from No to Yes. See his arm. But all I have is my No.

He won't leave.

That clergy woman with her brittle hair and her screen with bits of flesh on it.

Inside we have aspirin. If I gave him this with some words about how much water and a cross in the dirt for magic in this light, gold all day, not just at dusk like where I come from, motes hanging in the air all day in suspension like a drink of oil and water or drugs and water, maybe he will go and be happy.

But inside are the spiders and the dull thuds. I wish there were a window where I could see what is moving and thudding. Once in the night the wall did move with hard wings. You would look and look and whatever light— moon or fire—would shine on these wings, you would see them all together moving in their wall on the wall, and you would think the wall was moving.

Or are the thuds the suitcase opening and closing and is there smoke in that place without a window and does he fear the spiders and that is why he counts them even if they are only crawling along the inside of his head?

When you go quickly from the outside inside, the gold makes you not able to see. This is a blessing. I can't see what moves. I need aspirin, I say.

Out of the hot dark he hands me a box.

There are two men in that dark. There is this smoke. I hold the box.

Are you my bride? asks the man who wears no clothes.

Bride? I know the word. All day when I walk around men

say this because they want my color for theirs. I laugh at them because what should I do? Ask for their cows? Now I look down.

The CIA promised you to me.

I stop my look down, I stare. This is in my language.

Then I am not sure that CIA was it because he has so many teeth moved around and no clothes and he is in the dark and the smoke but I listen.

The man laughs. Without clothes on, the man makes this laugh go from his navel up to his mouth and back. At the end of the laugh, the man I am with does not say, She is mine, you can't have her. Or even, what CIA?

Very funny is what I say. I edge myself and my box toward the hole that is the door, trying to see the man sitting there, how he is wearing no clothes and knowing my language.

White is CIA, says the man who is with me after a long toke. Everyone who is white is CIA.

I nod. Of course.

Then he sings: I have spots on my cow. They see you, he sings, in their tune, the way they sing. He holds up his hands like binoculars are in them.

The man doesn't laugh.

You are my brother, he says, the man who is with me says to the naked man. He wiggles the nail he has in the hole under his lip. It is a magic trick, this wiggling, where people fall down to their knees and spit on his hands in the name of brother when they see it. It is instead of scars, the scars that let you marry or fight, that the other man has plenty of.

She is the one, the man says in the slow certain way of a person who is not impatient, or who is maybe showing off his English, or who doesn't really mean it.

I say, Excuse me and take the aspirin, just one tablet, in my hand, and crouch to the door and go through it.

He starts singing as I leave but I don't want to hear him. I prefer the counting and the dull thuds. I put the tablet in the man's hand who is waiting. I tell him the tablet is strong and it is the clergy wife who says this. I make up words and a certain kind of cross in the dirt.

He holds my hand, palm to finger. What he says is another bride proposal. I smile because I don't know what else to do with my face. Then there is the word oil—but from the singing inside which is now louder, which is angry, but in whose voice?

The man walks away, the one with the aspirin, his staff making a mark in the dirt behind him, his hand still around that pill that could powder and leave a trail back to me.

I make him walk away using my smile to say none of the words he uses can I use as mine.

Hey, he wasn't out any cows.

From inside, the voices go on past oil. In what language? Who cares since they don't bother to come out to see if I am here or not, to see if I am over a horizon which starts a hundred miles past my stuck out feet and clearly harbors dragons if not lizards at its edge and then what? Deserts are in all the stories and desert it is.

I could climb into one of the boats that are glued with mud in the bottom, with sides that show the hacking of a knife as ridged as the backs of the animals who float by the boat or lie in the sun on the shore while their young run over them on short legs, like dogs. I could use the boat to escape.

■

They come out in the dark.

I am talking to a woman then. We are talking until they come out. She has a sister with a belly like the woman who carries the little boy, who is well, I hope. A sister maybe not the way we are sisters, but how are we sisters anyway. By birth or by death? This sister will take a long time to die, she says, it is like bearing her death, she says with some bending at the waist and pointing at her belly. Then she says she is not menstruating now—that is how hard we are trying to talk. This is the dry season, she tells me, the time before the crops bear, there is no food for babies so why start? says the body, she says. It is not that she is pregnant.

She and I are stripping leaves off a branch from where in this flat, bare place? From some place far off—she bore the branch on her head out of the horizon that was darkening and stopped where I sat. The leaves are food. We have spice that come in leaves, why not food? But stripping a tree? That's a giraffe's way. No, she says, this is food for women, only women eat this. The men spit it out. She shows me how they spit it out, then she smiles.

It must be good for us.

She doesn't want to know, however, about the leaves that we eat or how I do this or that so I keep finding out about her. But even if she asks I don't want to tell her how we make our food. To speak of it makes that food farther away but the idea of it closer and troublesome.

I am closer now to here. Here, she is talking to me. I had no words I could use with the woman with the bad thing in her belly—her pain and my early Charlies did not go together. But like that woman, this one does not ask me to pound. My smile slides until it's mine and I do not have to make the face to say I'm not bad. Except for one joke where the middle finger gets chopped off, pretend, and reappears in the back of my arm, a ghost finger which mock-scares her and her quiet two children who sit almost on her feet while we talk. Then I make a face so they aren't frightened but laughing.

They startle me with their coming out.

You remember them, the man who has been here before and the one who knows English, who says I am his? They stand not too far away and talk in the dark. They shake hands. Who here shakes hands? What they do here is spit on each other's heads. Then these two don't turn to me, they don't take my arm and say Goodbye the way in the movies the heroine gets her last scene. He doesn't give me my pack and a kiss.

And I don't ask, What about me?

■

Of course he tells me all about it in the night. Night is different from day in how you tell things. Of course he tells me.

■

The woman is gone in the daytime. I ask about her with the name she gave me but no one says Yes. Or even No. In the afternoon I hear him say last night a woman and her children went by gunpoint back to the man who paid the cows for her and needs her to feed him. His brother had the guns.

Let that be a lesson maybe is what he is saying, what they are saying by not saying.

Sometimes if you throw a rock as high as you can down the river, really throw it, something will jump up and swallow it.

■

He tells me I am a big baby. Women in three-fourths of the world have babies without doctors or drugs or hospitals. Who would be here if it were not for these women, before those things? What a baby I am and what about free women who do what they want and don't have to be married to do anything? I turned him down, remember? I am not married, doing this, a free woman. What a baby I am to want to use these socks over his member. Just because I have lost the pills, because they are not to be found? This is like a Halloween mask, he says. Or a robber's. Let me have all your money, Mrs. CIA, it says in its raincoat.

I am laughing. Inside, I am wanting babies? I don't think that's what I am wanting with three-fourths of the women in the world. I do not say this at all to him but he knows, he knows I am at least making the question. He is pressing my thigh with the usual which is not in any raincoat.

Usually the pills lay at the bottom of the bag, enough for

a life of no births. Bullets to me, they were: Bang, bang, I'm not dead, I'm not pregnant in a place where it is dangerous to be. Is this like the gun on the table? But the pills are not there at the bottom when I go, as I do daily, not at the same time but similar, to grope in the dark to find them.

I am not laughing now. I am seeing a raft of these pills all joined in their plastic taking the river as a road, as a horizon, and who is at the other end, who, knowing what about the bottom of the bag? Still, he takes my You and makes me say Sorry, I didn't mean that, I know better and Yes, I do misplace things and now he's saying this one-a-day method is no good anyway, he says, it's vitamins you need.

What does thinking you're dying, I ask, have to do with having a baby? I know having a baby means you live forever, sort of. Someone to carry on your name. But what about the boy with your name? I ask, the boy with the fever, the son of the man you call brother?

He gives me a look which is not racist, which spells out how long his immortality bears on that child, that sick one, even at the missionaries, with the mother with the thing fixed, not even counting the father.

I haven't told about the father. His brother. So to speak. When we were there we slept on rubble, we saw the fish we spent the day catching go for drink, we drank because we couldn't eat. I couldn't look at the father. Even the cloth he wore across his shoulder like a toga, a sign of his important place or his money or at least his power, the knot he made in that cloth wasn't right, the knot slid down his shoulder at an angle that was drunk. The man who had been there before knew him from then. He was different then, he says to me. Someone gave him something after, he says. Why? or For what? I ask.

See, it happens to everyone, he says, as if age corrupts and not power. It was nothing. It could happen to me, he says.

I don't ask again about what changed him. What's the hurry about dying? is what I say.

His answer makes me say, But before we left and, Of course I believe and, But now. All that clouds up in the question which he doesn't answer before about the brother. Not the one with a gun but the one who wanted me. You can go with him if you think I am one of them, he says.

If his answer had been in frost, least likely in this place, it would have coated the inside of where we were in the netting in whiteness and stopped the air from its in and out and then my breathing. He had no reason to bring up that man. I had some belief.

■

If fish have engineers in their brains who pull the levers of in-water-out, we wear fish behind our ears when we board boats.

He could have said that to me but he is resting. I am watching the boat load. A fresh fear of boats means no rest for me. This boat stalled for two days in the no-fish, no-land zone of the swamp where papyrus is too high and too thick to carry on, and the people who were again so many had no food.

But now new people get on. And they get on. The size of the vessel is not the size of all those people, the size is the same as when we came and the netting is the same that did not stop the water but kept me in when so many people went to one side.

A man at the front of the boat has a pad and a pen and as each of the people goes on he calls out Hi in his language and puts a mark where I think a name should be. Hi, the way *aloha* is both hello and goodbye, both for now and when the boat is maybe sinking its last.

I am making up the Hi word to be more than it is but when I point at the boat where the water is coming in over the sides and back at those climbing on, more and more, I make my own Hi! Do people who are not me in many ways not care about this? Or is this swamp island so noisy they must leave, they are driven to leave even if the boat goes down before they get out? Hi I say, and say more.

He touches his fingers to the paper and says something that makes the people start to come out but then the ones who are waiting get on from the back. The loading is back and front now, with the getting off in the middle, but no fewer altogether in the people department.

He will die by water is what I put in my notebook. He will never film and the unshot film and camera will sink with him.

I do not throw any shot film in, even in my head. You can be the producer he says, you can worry about the film, not me.

He never looks like he naps. He looks now like he has been counting spiders. We are going behind those screens again, I say. I don't hold up my notebook where I put in about the water and his dying. I don't say how I tried to save him with my loud Hi!

We are not walking, he says with a stretch. You should like that. He has his lip nail in so his words are more like their language but I understand anyway without taking each sound and pounding it out, flattening it with a Charlie. I understand.

How is sex not like love? I ask.

I have just bought two eggs from someone who is walking across where we were walking, and the eggs, their tit-
tight shape which will soon be flaccid, direct my saying
this about sex and love.

He is not directed, though. He is moving a piece of cloth
over the front mirrored part of what he shoots with and

maybe the moving takes up every bit of his speech, maybe he is part of that mirror by reflection and liking it so much his hearing is less or maybe even some spider is making its way across the floor that he doesn't want to scare with an answer so it will not harm him. Or me.

I hold the eggs, one in each hand, as if I could break them by squeezing. I can't, though. The shape is special. Italians use this shape to say The Future because The Future is supposed to be simple and invulnerable and one in which you don't know which came first. The only thing here that is like that is sex, in relation to love.

Consider it a metaphor for all the rest, I say.

He's not a foot away, his ears must hear me.

Consider it Africa, I say. We take her daily, fuck, get fucked, but whose flag do we turn to? Who do we think spring, summer for?

There is throwing the eggs at him. There they are in my hands. But that is too hard to do when there are so few of them.

I think what we need is a dog, he says.

He says this with the cloth on his fingers and two fingers sticking up on either side. I have seen him with this cloth like this outside, with children, but I did it first, my cloth from my skirt, my animals. He is more clumsy. See how he puts the fingers together and mates them? Clumsy.

I get it, I say. I did not invent puppets. I invented love. As in, made up.

I put the eggs down and then I put them down again so they won't roll. All there is is dirt at a slant and the roll that is toward him.

I want that roll to say Here I am, I'm happy and This is

yours and I love you, a telegram of Yes, yes, yes. I don't
want to cut sex off love like a piece of tissue no one wants.
The people here I have heard do this with women but I
don't think so. I think the person who asked the question
did not get the question right. It is a matter of the question
and to whom? Like who knew how to ask dolphins, never
mind what. We think just because we're the same species
the questions and their making are right. No one who is so
modest in their no clothes, knees together, feet just so that
I find it impossible to do the same and am thus not modest,
has had this cutting happen to them.

What do I know?

He wants a dog.

I am not enough, I reflex. I scrub at a pot with grass. I
take water from the pot that I fill every day at a place in the
river that is farther than where I walk to do what you do in
the morning and I walk back with the water falling on my
feet because I can't walk with it on my head or I have to
begin again and again, I take this water and rinse the pot
and my fingers and wipe my face with that little water, and
because of the dirt and the morning sweat I don't mind the
food bits that stick to my cheek, not so much. What I mean
by the Not enough is not that there is not enough of me
after the finding and the cooking and the cleaning up after
food to do my work with the words and a dog would be too
much, but that there's barely food for two, only enough so
we count out everything in child portions. Of course I mean
enough to be about love and—why not?—loyalty, but
that's not the first thing.

How will I menstruate without enough food?

Dogs here get clubbed. They try for food on the baby's

face or where some other dog has dropped saliva waiting for a grain or shard of bone, and they have fights. This is why their fur shows holes. The fur comes brindled like the cows and their names, like the cows', are about that fur and those fights.

If I don't menstruate, how can I keep track of what's going on?

So I will be fighting with this dog. A puppy? I ask.

He moves his head up and down as he polishes the same way. To teach tricks to, he says. Fetch, roll over, pray to Allah.

The Arabs have puppies?

Yes. The puppies are under the truck and its spare parts and they just want to eat them.

Let's have sex, I say. The picture of the puppy on the grill is too suggestive for my hunger. I think of soft fur instead, what could be under me instead of cow. But warm. And loyal.

The Arabs are who saved us from the boat by having a boat on the other side of a chunk of swamp that we were behind and not moving from. The Arabs let us walk over that chunk, lightly like that swamp deer, and board their boat while the people in their boat walked over the chunk to our boat and boarded our boat and the boats just turned around and went back with new people, the ones who wanted to get here and there. The Arabs who saved us also own the truck and its parts.

It is quite big, the truck with the parts that take advantage of the sun and seem to grow to a size, but the inside parts don't grow as well and when other parts fall off they must be cast again after melting down spears for the metal. So it isn't as if there is any going with the truck. The Arabs wait for parts and train their dogs to eat flies by jumping face-height and snapping.

These are the dogs that have puppies. One set is tied to a post that holds up a barn, all of them loud at the end of yellow thongs, getting thinner and thinner until the mother, who is also tied, eats one and then two. The other set is under the truck, the part that is not on the ground. Two people lie under there too, a crowd, these two with their tea and their carpets for prayer, and these two like the dogs at night in the cold but not by day when the dogs share the shade and make it more hot under the truck, panting.

We have a dog from under the truck.

The dog becomes us quickly. That is, it is not like the Arabs' dogs who jump and lounge and ignore the Arabs except for the flies they snap, and not like the dogs who live here that get clubbed trying for food and so become curs, but like ours, the ones that follow and wag tails and whine when food doesn't come quickly.

The dog is now tracking up my lessons because he wants my attention, another us thing, but my attention is all on the people who have come to trade songs for their names. Today they all want to know how to write their names and so I do my best with a stick in the dust, making the letters go together, saying *cieng* for sun for the open *o* and the word for rat when we need a tail. In the dust all around me lie the names of the people who have come to learn and their children, who are making more names with sticks. It's just the dog that doesn't like it, that walks through it all and gets clubbed.

I find it wonderful, all this script everywhere. The why of it I find out later. Almost all my cassettes are filled at once with songs in exchange. This is not to say that my pages of finding words for the songs in my language are just as full—they are mostly lace, though now and then I try to put more down, wiping the chuff of my hand over and over to get off sweat, and using very hard lead. But I've come to rely on the cassette as a way to change the words to mine. After I put them in the notebook I say what I write into the cassette before the notebook gets eaten into air.

A woman comes sometimes to help me find the words to do with sex which sound like something else and corrects them so the songs make sense. Entendre often doesn't make sense. Sometimes she talks to me too, and pinches my nipples and says, What a shame, no babies. She has this sadness because no babies to her and all the women here means at least a divorce, and maybe a still to run or maybe the making of witch things for the rest of life, or maybe suicide. This is what this other lady told me, the one who left in the night in front of her brother-in-law's gun, so it is true. This woman feels how small my nipples are under my shirt and shakes her head, but they are not broad and brown like now. She has not been coming by for some time. He said something to her and she doesn't come by anymore, he says maybe, I like your nipples too. So when she comes today to have me help her make her signature, all the letters walking together, I am surprised, I am happy.

My breasts have spread, turned brown like butter burning so fast I'm not sure I'm not sick. Maybe it's how I become the people here. I know a few words, and some places on me get brown, and then more. It's not that I stand around in the sun. I stand around wherever to get words. The more I know the fewer I know because they speak faster, so getting brown here probably is just my cells trying to catch up. To the woman who helps me I try to say *Egen*, Yes, because I know she hates Charlies, but this time she doesn't pinch me so I can show her my brown, where it circles my nipples, she is so excited to make her signature all her words go even faster past me. What I think I hear is that she has a paper and will bring it to put her name on.

Paper? People here smoke paper.

Then she says in words and a speed that is all right with me, that the Arabs will take any land that does not have a paper and a name, that they are coming to take this land, although take is puzzling to her, does someone come and peel it up?

I understand about the names now. And the little scraps, the almost-artifacts of paper that some of the ones who come to learn bring with them, how the paper could be part of that, and, of course, not part of that, wrong.

The dog is wiping the names off everywhere with his big tail and feet and the children are beating him like it's a game he likes, when he comes back, the one who has been here before and who has been Where? He sees all the names and I say, Is this about oil?

He says, The Arabs want the land for oil. I'm document-
ing the last of these ways before the change.

I nod, I make my head go up and down.

There's a problem, he says, and takes my machine from
me.

Oh?

He needs to fix the machine I use.

I don't know there is a problem with that machine, I was
just using it, but he is good at fixing things and will do it
easily. Although soon I am not sure, there are many more
pieces than ever of the machine, more than I thought could
be inside such a small black box lying in the dust next to
where he is working.

There, he says finally. I can't do it.

But nothing was wrong with it, I say, my hands out like
they have something to do with its right or wrong. My
hands start to shake when I pick up the parts. I am not good
with parts. And there is all this dust on the parts.

I sit until dark moving the parts together and not. Some
of them fit and some never. Is there a missing piece or is
there something bent? This is nothing I know. And it is
hard with the dark coming on and the way my eyes keep
clouding with water which must be liquid anger because it
is not sad I am feeling.

To travel with someone who knows the way but who is
not someone you are with is a problem. The man with the
map on his back, for instance, is still a man. How would it
be to go with him? How far did he take us once—four days?
And four nights. All that has to go backward and more
before I get anywhere out.

Does he know how much I want to leave him? I am the

only one in this color who can speak this language that no one else knows here, who has seen the place where his berries grow and buildings fall behind balls, the only one who thinks the oil that he knows about has something to do with the writing in the dust all around me.

I wait, like a snake in the wall. I wait like a woman in an adventure story, a female adventure story where adventure is not me against all the others and odds, each moment a resolution directed toward some big burst, but an experience of motion, the two browns of my nipples both questions that bear me to what I know all along, if I remember everything in an order that makes sense, not that comes one after the other.

If I learn whistling from him, it is like owing the mother for milk. I don't have to pay.

Besides, I have brown nipples. I can change.

Why won't I look? He is holding a leaf between his teeth and the animal is leaning down and taking the other end of the leaf and they are both tugging, but I won't look. He says he will get the animal to kiss him and still I won't look. There is a moment when I hear the leaf resist, dry as it is, and it tears, then something quiet happens.

I am looking and not looking. My eyes are still not clear

from when they were clouded with water that showed my anger. And I am uneasy about being so close to animals who have, I hear, sharp hooves and clearly such height. But walking in front, I don't see them until he stops and has the leaf in his mouth and is whistling low so they can understand him.

I really don't see them.

He says I can't look because I am jealous. Look at this kiss, he says, and picks up another leaf. But it is not the grey-black mass of a tongue that is moving down the leaf toward his hair-rimmed opening that is why I can't look, not even the softness of the sound, something he rarely applies to our kissing. To see him tender and funny is too hard to watch.

Is he or isn't he tender? Amazing how, day to day, the is doesn't matter, the mattering is all next-meal-hunger, all how to get away from that hunger. For this job he may or may not have a good worker should be given enough food so this tenderness doesn't matter to me who distrusts, who doesn't know.

If he had something growing on his front, maybe I would not look too. But I think I would. I would try to help or change this place on his front even if he is in their employ. I have this reason, love, something you can't see. These animals I don't see come out of the flat plainness of this place, making it gaudy with their spots of soft brown, they simply walk into my looking into the emptiness all around them. A trick of light? What trick does he have? I bolt, the way they do later when I drop the bottle of water. But how far to bolt?

I think about my back. I don't know if he has some kind of gun that has bullets that would stop me in the back. I don't want to look into his pack even if he doesn't want me to look and he is the only one who is looking because without looking I can think it is love and not a gun that keeps me.

This love is what we don't use when we talk. Maybe we do for a while, that while before we came here, those months after meeting, when going here was a way to fire what was between us into a unit, into something to use. That love is in the pack?

It's not about the kiss that I should be jealous but this show of softness that bends what I think I know of him, that makes me not want to look, that's confusing. His silliness works against what is in the clouds behind my eyes and what is in the pack or not, all of which I want to keep straight, in case.

All he has to do is say he has something there. He doesn't have to get it out. He doesn't have to catch me looking. He hasn't said it yet but I know that will be all he has to do. He says love but when that isn't enough, he says how he will die soon. He doesn't have to cry, he doesn't have to kiss tall animals or share their leaves.

How do I know about the gun? There is the pack that is his and he packs it, not me, never me. And lumps lump up in his pack which look solid, not like the sheet which we don't have since the missionaries, nor the things that he smokes in the suitcase. But I don't know. Not knowing is the same as knowing this time—like love's not knowing. But it could be a shoe, an extra shoe he is carrying.

I am saying, Does the length of a tongue show how much it must tell the truth? Like the reverse of the nose-length that is lying? I am saying this while the animal's dark ropey tongue snakes down the leaf toward him again and when I let the bottle slide out of my slick hands. Then the animals cut hard into the ground with knife clicks made by their hard-heeled hooves. I watch them go, that looking is not hard—they are free.

He asks why I wouldn't kiss them too. Does he mean I am not kissing him enough? He watches me think of answers.

This answer should not be too hard or he will begin to think I am thinking other things. The waiting for the answer says something, like to the clergy. I bring out a laugh instead, it is what I have anyway because he is asking me this with his lips still pursed as if by kissing him I will have kissed them too anyway.

It is a question of competence.

He can't have this job because he is not competent. We didn't even begin to walk until the sun is already up today so we can't go far. Is this what he wants? He says he must meditate in the mornings. Does he mean triangulate, something to do with land and the way he stands with his arm out? But he is better when he starts later, he has this tenderness. But competence? He called one of the men by the name of his cow instead of him. And he smokes what he has in his suitcase. I have to laugh. Competence must not be a requirement. All my ideas of this job start with what? Oil and people with papers and his anger? And being a bride to someone? Everyone of our color and place in the world here will get these questions, as he says.

If you come to me with a leaf, I might kiss you instead, I say.

He finds four leaves. Then we walk. The dog walks behind us, the dog who didn't see the animals until I did, another way he is like us? Or just me?

So if I have a problem with trust when we begin to walk, I have just more of a problem now. And one more thing: I am making these songs into my language for money, and some of the money I have given him to buy film. Some is more like a lot. That is why he calls me Producer. All along when we set up the camera, I expect the lights, camera, action, at least the red light inside the camera that says it is going, taking the looking. He should make the camera go on even if he has this job, to make me think he does not. But then the action happens, with all of its like-life things, and sometimes it even unfolds in front of the camera, like babies dying from burns they get from rolling into fires at night, cold nights, and he does not make the light go on.

Maybe the baby will die again, I say.

That isn't the subject, he says. But what subject is there? I ask but not very loudly. It is a mistake to ask as if someone might want the answer, especially if he doesn't want to give it, he wants to talk about it.

It would be easier if he just didn't look, if he just turned on the red light, lay the box with the red light on its side and let it run, I say. It would do away with perspective, I say. It would make it more objective and scientific. No one could accuse you of point-of-view.

I have to put the camera somewhere, don't I? That means I'm pointing. It's not right, he says. It shows me off and not them.

Oh, boy, I say. How did you do this before?

I was the eye before, the first time. I was their eye. Maybe it will happen again.

My respect does not leak away with the pronouns. I must say I like his way of not looking. It has an argument. But how long does it take not to look? And sometimes do you never look?

Now, if he can find the ones who paint themselves blue, he says, that will make him film.

That is why we are walking again. Why I am walking with him. With love too but with a kiss that is too hard to reach so often. We are walking for blue people who have skin that the film needs for its starting and songs I should not miss. When, of course, the machine has all its parts and a way of going together.

Sometimes it is fixed. Sometimes when whoever is walking in front of us walks off to see if there are people who are not his cousins and might kill us camped nearby, he finds a way to fix it. I think he has a part he puts in. The cassette which is not yet turned into an egg he puts in after he puts in the part that has our music on it and it comes out of his pack which I do not ever open.

Last night I was saying, Turn the machine off. Not because I am angry that I have not been able to take more of their songs and make them mine, oh, no, I could use a break—I agree with him, or at least it is his idea that I could use a break and that he thinks I'm working hard makes me happy—it is because I am in my husband's arms with that music, a song with my husband's arms playing me as his guitar as all men of that music had guitars and girlfriends with breasts they played. It is not that the music reminds me of the husband who is not one now, not now for some years—which does not make me old, just rash— it is that it reminds me of feeling. Of how I don't want it. As long as I can skip feeling, I don't mind the loyalty I use, the let me count the ways we can't be someone else when my clothes are off. Music, with its high and low tempos, its organ-swollen words that promise you or him to each other, is too much. Mixed with warm air in the night, that blackness behind that holds it, it is where there could be husband, and feeling.

I look out at the hot flat land I am on now. In this season, you have to use an axe to make a hole in this dirt. No one dies and gets a hole now. The dog sniffs and stirs if he finds a hole because there is only one thing that makes a hole in this hot flat land and that is a fish thick with fat up and down in that hole. It must be pulled out, inched out once the dog and then dogs are beaten off, and when the slick fish is out it doesn't die. It writhes even as it is put in the fire and you think if you peel off its black scales and skin you will find it still that way, writhing. Instead, the meat is orange and so sweet.

That is the past. Plenty of air holes to the present. Even jokes, holes in the arid air. Here's a joke: my not feeling.

You will be my bride, that man said. I feel the spittle of bride on me from his carefully spaced teeth. I have felt it once before and did not know what was happy.

When you walk you do not get farther away from before. You walk through it over and over, until even the time you are walking is from before, even the foot you put out in front is the past because it is already happening and has happened in your head.

Soon we will be there, he says. We will beg the man in charge to take us with him in his jeep. Maybe he has to go kill some blue people because they are not happy with him. Or he has to get some others there with guns to help the blue people relax. That is what he is hoping, and it is what the man who is looking for people who are not cousins hopes. A relaxing trip is what we all hope.

It must be soon though. A shelf of cloud, a grey length of plywood, mirrors the hard flat land, and it darkens daily, it hangs a little lower each day and once cracks and soaks somewhere so far off it is like the husband in my arms with the music, that far off. But it will tear closer, it is nailing itself closer and closer, and when it comes that plywood will fall for some months.

When it is that wet, he says, you can't walk, the wet sticks and grows on your feet with each step. Clay feet, he says, No cliché, he says. You could make Bakelite, he says. We could be stuck with blue people up to our ankles.

I feel my breasts, my brown-tipped breasts. They are the only part of me with roundness. I feel them and wave to the women who are passing with long box baskets on their heads. From inside these baskets come cries and from the outside, singing. The women are shaking rattles and singing very loudly so the babies can hear only them and not their crying. I wish I could fix the machine myself with some part I had so I could put these songs and the crying on the tape. But maybe the women wouldn't stop and maybe I wouldn't make them stop and I would just think about it.

If I were an airplane, the babies would look up at me from inside the baskets, these crying babies wondering about all that singing. If I were an airplane, I would see a woman with breasts under her shirt watching them, stopped and watching, with the dog going on, the men going on. I would blink red, not as a warning but in greeting, to get her to look up at her past, watching over her watching, because planes are from before. Then she could look up or just wonder at my shadow making lines across the whole land until they run off together in perspective.

They do end but you can't see it.

So much depends on not seeing. I didn't see the animals and so my walking showed no stopping which the animal could see and warn them about me. Instead, they were standing there as if waiting and the tree they were eating still had some leaves on it that he could use to make the tall ones bend down and kiss him.

I must look and see if it is love I can do without, or blue people. And I must look into his backpack. I must see what it is that is waiting, even if it is hard to look.

The soon is relative, he says in the dark without a flash-light—because where would we get new batteries here?— the dark with half a moon.

We have to pole upriver with the equipment this time. Against the current.

I am not as sad as I could be with the delay. I see Cleopa-

tra, a smart black woman, on a barge and leaves at the end
of branches waving over me. Mostly, I see no walking.

I don't ask where exactly will this be, where we are
going, just the way I didn't ask where exactly did he leave
the money. He should not know I want to know exactly.
My finding out has to be from someone else. It is like the
way I don't ask him about the gun that I did once sleep
against which had no shoe shape.

But it's water you're afraid of, I say.

The river is shallow now that it is so dry. We could wade.
But don't you want to go in a boat?

A boat leaves no footprints is what I don't answer.

A satellite blinks through some chinks. I am not lost, at
least I see satellites. I am just not found, not looked for.
Maybe he has some small silver something like a bug sewn
to the inside of his pack that makes him found to the ones
who employ him and watch him. But at least then they're
watching, which is more than stars do. For that reason, I
like to watch satellites better, although probably some have
weapons which, of course, I can't see.

We are sleeping inside a tent of cornstalk, each stalk
leaning into the next, a lean-to the cows haven't eaten yet,
or leaned-into. But there are no cows around here—this is
a fishing place or so says the man who leads us past and
through cousins who like him and hence us.

He is smoking page 132 and I am glad the slim book I
thought right for camping is the fat one I thought I'd never
read anywhere else. But burning money! All the extra cassettes are now filled or gone so I worry about my exit,
exactly how many pages will take me back when I have my
courage and my songs together.

What is together is the dog and myself. He is shove and push but pillow, because he is warm. The dog watches if we put ourselves closer, my fat chest against the man's, he watches with more interest than if we eat. Is he jealous or confused, the way I was confused with the giraffe and the kissing? Love and sex are dog things too.

The man with the cousins sleeps on the door side of the fire. How do you think people keep on having more? this man who has been here before whispers. They don't have guest bedrooms.

I don't think I have that question about these people. I hug the part that's all dark, that could be someone else's, but is so silky.

■

The birds fight over which one should shit on us. He says they're dropping close to see if we have fish but that is the end so I question the means. The size of the birds and their interest makes me think they also want dead meat. That's soon me: the sun against the water hurts my skin and bores through my eyes to an ache in the back. At least the birds' swooping makes a kind of shade.

Poling is rehearsal for hell. Aren't there waters in hell that push you backward? Backward is relative, yes, like soon, like soon you will die, why keep on? the water only wants to go the other way. For me, the water pulling against the poles has the pull of escape. If I go that way, I can only end up out. Every pole put down says Yes, I am going on to finish and not go out, I can do it.

I don't think about the boat being coffin-shaped. I do

think how, if I move, I will fall in, and even with the falling-in nice, the water more cool than the blood in my body, there's still the usual problem, just in shallower water.

I would think they would be fat now with all the fish so close together.

He says no, they just get an appetite.

I suck on a tablet for killing what the mosquito leaves to make myself think it is a gin and tonic in my mouth. I use my imagination.

The dog doesn't move. Like the boat doesn't move, he scoots forward to pant over the prow, then sucks in his muzzle fur with his breath and slumps to the boat bottom. And again.

It is the time for idle questions because he can't sleep all the time, sometimes he must pole. They won't let me pole, at least not in the maze with the cousins who might not like us. So while he is poling, I talk.

After a while I say, In case you die, where did you put the money? I ask this apropos of nothing, of the backward and forward of our talking. He puts the pole in, pulls it out and says he left the money with the husband of the woman with the something on her belly.

The one who drinks so much we have nothing to eat there? But I don't say that, I nod like that's a good idea. I look out and down the river that must lead somewhere back to them and out because no one could live away from it. It is my road of the future, with or without him. It is what I could take any time and glide right to the doorstep, to the money. If there is any.

I discount some of the things I know and don't like, like

the big By myself? or the big When? for I am bleeding now in what is called a cycle which I thought for some time would not happen because of the dog making no food for us and all of these sicknesses which I don't mention.

We will stay with someone I know, he interrupts my discounting. While we are getting permission from the police to go on the trip to relax the blue people.

He says this someone is like us, this someone is white.

And no one, like us, I don't say. Yes, they spit on our heads in happiness but after that, except for when he takes out the camera and feints with it like a gun, we could be our own zoo. No, that is too much looking. Only the children look, for example under my shirt to see if my breasts match the rest. For everyone else we are only white mouths that who wants to watch? I see this when the chicken of the cousins of the man who is leading us is cooked and we get the head, the best part, and they can't watch us eat.

To see someone who has eaten that part of the chicken who is like us will help.

■

It is three airplanes in reverse to get out, I say. I am mushing the fish, a way of breaking small bones and finding the big. Fish like this is good with couscous and next I am adding a little water to flour and rolling—with one hand only—the pellets of couscous.

He is drinking something marked 23 that is brown with gold when it's sloshed and set down, which is not often. This is the man we are staying with. The other is walking around in the dark for appetite? As if he has lost something or would like to.

The three airplanes hum on their strip in my head while I mush the fish, while he says So? and then, Why don't you come with me?

He means it, though the 23 slows the words. I have known him for two hours and because of the place we are in, I believe he means it. And he is engaged to someone who is in a picture folded in his wallet that he has shown me, which means he would just escort me to the first plane, and wave.

I say, Well.

He comes in from outside now. For the celebration, he says. All the explorers had their something, he says. Livingstone opiates, Burton boys. He opens his suitcase and rolls and rolls, exclaiming: Tomorrow! They'll give us permission tomorrow! Blue people!

The drunk man does smile. As blue as the river you came on.

That's black at most, I say. More brown.

It's in the clay, the man who's inhaling says with his big breath. The river banks show blue everywhere because the water is so little. Everyone will be blue.

The drunk man is still smiling. I study the people, he says. They're my people. I know their blue. Good luck.

I get the picture, he says, smoking. Your people. You don't think we should see them.

It's not me, the drunk man says. You'll see.

Silence fills up the rest. The man I came with works his mouth more but not with words. Maybe with anger.

See how chicken she is with her neck? he says to him after I go to the door and throw bones out like there is no anger between them. The ladies call her hair chicken but I think it's her neck. See?

When I step back, he fits his hands around my neck in a cuff of fingers, a tight cuff that he is tightening. I am smiling like he likes my hair, isn't that nice? because it is a kind of attention, because it changes the anger of before.

The drunk man comes over and pulls the other man's hands away from my neck and before I can smile a Thank you, he says, It isn't much, and fits his own hands that are shaky with drink around, tight and loose, as if measuring.

Tears pop into my eyes. I work this fish mouth of mine around words so they don't say tears. The man I am with turns away, smoking, not watching. The drunk man laughs and gives my neck a shake. Why don't you have some? He offers the 23 which makes his hands free of me.

I do. I drink.

She wants to remember everything, says the man who is with me but not. She won't drink.

I drink.

Women, says the drunk man.

How much of the woman in the picture is he loving? I want to ask. Is that a picture he shows to all the women who come here? But how many come here?

The 23 is making the smoke wave.

Yes, she's in love with me, he says, eating the end of his smoke, sitting up. She remembers everything about me. In darkness and in health, he says.

The other man snickers, a sound which is all by itself.

I brush the fish off my hands and I go out into the dark

to work on my songs. I have a line in my head which is missing a word, my new way of using my head instead of the cassette or the paper. It is all I can think to do, this smelling my hands and shaking and listening. I listen for the word outside in the moonlight while I throw more fish bones into the river to keep them from the dog who gets them anyway. I won't stop him. I eat even the tail.

Later, because I have to come in, because I can't stand under stars waiting for sleep with animals out, and here there are no women all together in one place where I could go, where I could go if I were a true translator and not a coward with women and thinking I am loving him, no, here this is civilized, here I hear women being beaten somewhere. I turn, away from the river, I think, and then I turn again, where the path must be. My bare feet don't think so though, and they walk to where we caught the fish in the morning, a cliff and a turn where fish hesitate and think food, because it is somewhere, and in the black I hear a cock.

I know this sound just from the movies. The metal goes against metal. It is not part of what frogs do which is most of the sound here. This is a cock, it says, and I stop. Do I turn around?

The cock is not far away and not really behind. It's at the side. I see the shine of it even in this half moon, and his eyes.

Hello, I say in their language.

I am military, says the someone with the gun that is cocked, who says it in English.

Okay, I say. That's African, the word Okay. I am the white woman, I say.

The gun goes up and down like a Yes, what else in this dark? The gun says it is still cocked.

I smell more of that 23 I left behind in a breath from where the gun is. I say, I'm going now. Back. Tomorrow, maybe we will go together, I say. To where the blue people are.

The gun seems to smile as I see the someone with it smile. Tomorrow, he says, and is still cocked.

Okay, so the lion is stuffed. A smaller animal is running between her ears with straw, and a stick keeps her head up. I have come a long way to see a lion stuffed with straw, I say.

It was shot where it stands, he says.

That doesn't scare me, I say.

Behind the animal is a police station, a place almost as

leaning as it is, the straw corners that make the walls like the lion's corners are rounded too, like all the other places near it.

At this museum I know, I say, there's a sign that says the female is the hunter but the stuffed female below the sign is just watching the young. You can't ask them to take the straw out and re-stretch the jaws around the prey, can you? And not to kill another female.

He will give us permission, he says, and goes toward the door.

I like this motion, this going toward where we will film, and him doing it. In the daytime I like being the person along, the producer, the one with the film in front, who prods. Though, right now, the way we are moving he has me in front of him, like I am protecting him from what?

The man at the door has no gun, just a stamp pad. He holds the stamp in the air over the pad to get a fly. When the fly dies, the place where he missed the pad says PASSED. As in passed away, I decide.

I like his desk.

The man I am with pulls out papers from his pack. I have seen these before. They come written in Arabic with many names at the bottom which are less easy to read than the ones made in dust around me that day which seems farther away than the river's beginning. Police like to hold this paper for a while and then stamp it. What we are waiting for is that raising of the stamp and its falling on our paper.

He orders tea.

Is it racist of me to say everyone has no color now? It is not the suntan I have nor his features that are more like mine than not, if I ever had a way to look at mine. It's that if everyone else has color, then I am the same. Not conforming, just head logic, body logic. I don't even want the color because it is already mine.

Now, in this falling-down place with the lion in front, I want this man, this one with the stamp, I want him to tell me about his cows, about how the cows will buy him into my body. Maybe it is the smell of paper, all these filmy, bug-eaten papers that scatter from the door to the many places where straw is coming out, maybe because I like paper I like him, but the feeling is strong. Did I want the man who has my color, or the drunk one who measured my neck like this?

I also like his eyes. Brown and round and at a slant but not too yellow in the whites where they show a person's illness. I am running my own eyes all around all over him, putting a life into this room with the papers, a life of two, with the body before me who smiles at me, who is putting teaspoon after teaspoon of sugar into a small glass stuck with flies. I want to put my hand between the stamp and the paper and get the word put on my hand and not the paper that tells us we can go now. I don't want to go now. Not even for the blue people or my money, or to save these people from the oil that must run under here like a black river, the negative of the one we pole down.

It is not a matter of color.

I hold the hot tea until it is not. I say many words in my language because he knows them from the Bible, and making them makes me lean closer to him until I can see in the place between buttons, flesh.

When no one is wearing clothes, there is no looking. With clothes, you look. With just a toga like the man who lived with the woman with the thing on her belly, and our money, you looked in case the wind took the cloth and parted it. With actual buttons and actual sewing, you look at the seams like they are pointing, you look at where they come together. Here, with this heat, that is the purpose of clothing. Not the purpose that the clergy thought, bringing clothes to cover up and forget, clothing which has the need for soap which needs money which no one needed before and if you don't get it, what gets between the skin and the clothes itches, then pusses, then kills you. So it might as well point.

I am telling him my father has cows, I come from a place that is as flat as this, where the clouds add up and the sun is this bad but for only part of the time.

Her father will send the cows on an airplane, says the man I am with. He has made a smile curled up at the edges, which turns smirk.

We all make our laughs.

A boy comes to take the glasses away. Tell them to make food, says the man with the stamp. We are coming.

Food! I am walking as close to the man as I can. I even try to think how I can get rid of the man I am with and have the food just with him. It is so hard to even make a picture of that in my head that I smile.

We walk past the lion that can't move, we walk to a place that is like all the other places here, but with a long, tall cornstalk fence. Now this is civilized, this fence, though it doesn't keep lions from coming in, it does keep people apart and not knowing what each has.

But what does he have that he needs such a fence?

A woman stands in front of each of the ten round places,

a woman with a few or many children. Some of the children are small and crying and wetting themselves, others play with mud toys as strong as stone, cows with long curly sharp mud horns and humps, and some spear at a hoop or dance with mud dolls in a daze, pretending. They all look like him. Like a stamp.

I have all my wives on a schedule, he says.

For a moment all the women rush him. For a moment they love him, all of them, all of them run to touch him, to feel his lips and hands on them, his eyes. And I am going to be one of them, swept up, not responsible for what I am going to be doing with my lips and hands. It is like a pop star, I think, all these women coming toward him with their lifting of brooms and waving, one with a gourd full of milk that spills as she stumbles, one with a knife which she swings as she gets closer.

He steps back, he covers his beautiful head as the blows come down. He says many things in their language that I don't know and speaks it too quickly for me to make them out, especially now that he is leaving, hands over head.

Stay, he shouts as he backs away from the fence, they will feed you.

We stay.

He asks, What happened?

I don't want to know. I want to follow him down that cornstalk fence, its woven rows, apologize for this terrible error—they didn't meant to do that, please come back. I want him mine.

When they answer, they answer in bunches, in ways that even I understand, all together. They say he has not put the cows up for the last wife and he is looking at another and because of this, they say in an almost collective breath, they will not feed him, they will not sleep with him until he puts up the cows.

I like that he is still looking. I like them too, the way they are working together. And then, maybe because we are all drawn to him, or maybe because they're serving food already, I like them more. In a competition, women always like to serve food, the way my mother puts out fancy jello when women come over for cards.

Before we can dip our fingers into the eggs, the soft couscous, the single bird heart in the middle of a white plate that comes from where? he takes me away. He says, Did you see all those kids? To eat there would lower the IQ of an entire generation. Besides, we have to leave soon, we have to pack so we can film.

Film?

I would jump up to show how happy I am that he is taking an interest but I am sad to leave the man with the stamp and his wives, not to mention the food. That man is bad, but not so bad. Does the man who is with me suspect me and this man, my interest?

I am also not jumping because I am still bleeding. I am trying not to let him know this because he will want to take off what he is wearing on his member when he comes into me, saying he can stop the bleeding easily. He will want to do this and I will not and there will have to be more talk, and then more talk about how he is going to die. This bleeding I have is like writing, an ink that says something.

■

I imagined it all, I say to the man who is not drunk now, who rolled into my arm in the night and swore, thinking I was some animal, who is now taking a first drink.

The lion, the women. Did you like the story?

Outside, people are collecting. The boat in the swamp is a guide to how many. They stand or sit with their guns or their guns, and a few clothes, shoes here, shirt. They collect around the truck, which is small, really just space for coolers and dogs in another hot climate, maybe an old chunk of motor or some chain. A lot of them collect with their guns around the small truck, whoever cocked at me in the dark, and the man I am with among them.

I make up stories to make me feel safe, I say. The part I don't want to remember I say I make up, I say. I am light-headed because no one has found any food, I say. We could go back to the place with the women, and we laugh, and the almost drunk man watches me closely.

Of course you know the man with all the wives, with the stamp and permissions. And you probably shot the lion yourself, I say.

He takes another drink of 23 and puts three or four more 23s in his suitcase and walks away from me until he is small in the distance. He says as he leaves his girlfriend is three airplanes away too, and that's the problem. He says he is sick and that I will understand.

It's true I didn't say Yes in the night to go with him. He passed out before I could find my Yes, and today, telling him about the man with the stamp, seeing these women who had this man, I wanted him to say Yes for me without my asking, for my story. That way my leaving would not be my idea and I could stand behind him when the man I am with is looking through his pack, looking for what I know is there. Forget my neck in his hands, forget who is drunk. It's the one who is not drunk whose hands I try to make into a story. I want so much to go that his puzzlement after I make the question myself, his saying What? will make me cry and that is trouble because, after all, they were the ones who fell asleep together, not me with him, arm over arm, just me in the end against them.

I weep after his suitcase is as small as the fly that troubles the edge of my mouth. But the tears are not for me I decide, not frustration, but for the bleeding, tears of relief, of joy. I pack my pack. I pat the dog and give it four ants I find of a good size and watch him play under/over paw and lick.

No dog, he says. The dog has finished the ants with one swipe of the tongue and is now jumping and barking at all the ones with guns who come to the door.

Where will the dog go? I ask in a voice that I use in my head about this for myself. He says someone will feed it and I say Who? but the truck is honking already, all the guns go upright in the back with the men, and we hurry on between the guns.

The dog runs after us until it sees something, food I hope, and gets lost.

Like us. Who is driving but a lackey of the man with the most metal on his shirt, a man who knows only Yes in his language to match the metal. Yes is what he says starting out, Yes over here and Yes over there. But there is no road here. There is a river which we do not always follow,

which is not always where we are going, just ruts sometimes.

I'll bet the man with the suitcase of 23 just walked to
the place where you go in the mornings and will drink,
and wait.

The killing starts. By the way the weapons fall from the truck when the truck stops for stretching, I can see they don't kill much, not with these weapons anyway, with knives on the end which, when the truck bumps, some get hurt on. We don't always bump, sometimes the ruts fit the truck but rarely, as this place with no road is not a place for trucks to come much, even if they have shocks, which this one must not, so people need stretching, need to stop. When we stop and the guns fall to the ground with the men getting out all at once, the sound is like a lot of clubs dropping, heavy thuds to the dirt, clubs which they used to use but now don't. They use these now because the animals are quick, the man beside me says. But haven't they always been quick, these animals? The people who live here would have starved at the start if what they had before didn't work, I say.

He smiles. He checks to see how many bullets.

I have seen the bend in a boy's side after he throws one of the weapons they used to use, spears, boys who still make this bend with their bodies, the open *o* bend, how they make the shape of unfinished sound, the one the animal finishes. This kind of bend takes some practice to get good at so you know when to change the bend fast toward where what is running is going, in fear. But there's no bending with this other kind of weapon. You just point it and put out holes. Now boys who used to practice bending on passing birds or fish all day while the cows ate behind them, make clay guns that match the shine and the size of the ones that I sit with, that the ground has now, and these clay guns shoot wadded up grass with a pop. A pop of this type would have a better chance of hitting a hundred of these animals that look up out of the dust than the aims of those who have dropped their weapons into the dirt and have to pick them up and point them while the animals turn their rumps, the animals who must have heard the dropping to the ground through their feet. But what can they hear now with such loud sounds all around, so many weapons putting their holes into the air wherever? Still, one of the animals tilts with a hole but keeps on, one falls after a quick dance.

Why doesn't he bring out his gun to do the killing too? He doesn't want them to know about his gun, I decide. I still have this dull feeling, all hunched up, not yet with a hole inside. But I am bleeding already, with blood that is not a defeat but a triumph, a freedom from him. I have said nothing to him about this blood and walk with the others to where the one that has danced and is dancing lies.

Not enough blood, they decide. With a slice of what is attached to the end of their guns to the neck, just a slice, there's enough. Forget drinking it though. Nobody's brought a cup, they complain, and nobody sucks. Or splashes, as the situation is presenting itself. A shame, someone says, the way I've heard people talk after ruined gravy. Or is it shame about how it was killed?

The straddling happens. The animal loses its coat and lies in the real nude for the flies, for the dull chops and slashes of the ones who want dinner. Of course, that is me too. But for the slashing I have no stomach. Same of the animal's is being removed with its so very green chyme— the grass of dinner mixed with inside-the-body juices— tumbling to the dirt for the big birds who unfold their wings just above us, levering down their legs in the gold of the settling dust.

Who do they know who wants a head? They talk with each other. They wipe their hands on grass and their guns— there's no water, the head is facing the water with its blank headness, its eyes open with water in its balls, plus surprise. They only know that someone must want a head. Someone sets his feet apart over the head, where the head and neck hook, although how can you tell just where this is when there's such a smooth space from shoulder to head? This man puts a hand to each horn and twists.

I'm not saying you haven't heard this—chalk on a board, ratchets pulling wrong, even cars stripping at forward. But you haven't heard it this close to your own head with the sound filling your bones in your ears like your own sound. That is how you get a head.

The death of something I have seen before, having eaten often. And it is not as sad as I thought, except in transition when there's a lot of surprise on the part of the creature, the surprise of surprise. Yes, there's a twitch that the meat makes on bumps that crawls up the sides of my hands, and yes, the warmth of the flesh under where I sit adds to the warmth of the men who, with their weapons, sit more than shoulder to shoulder now as we bump away, and yes, the head is sad, left, no one takes it but the birds and maybe the animal that makes its peculiar dog-gallop to the bird-thick spot. In the end, no one wants the head in his lap, looking back at its bones as we bump, not even me who loves the eloquent spareness of the skull and its horns, the echoing of destiny and flowery words that the skull brings up, and its place as a hat hanger in every home. It is too much like my own head, my own eyes looking.

The trophy should be dog, he's the competitor.

I think I can still see the dog as a lump in the view that we face, going backward. But I stop thinking that when someone else sees this lump and lets his gun lose more bullets into the space behind us, the view.

■

I get out with the rest to rest. They light cigarettes, these people with weapons, fire with fire, though they don't use the pages of novels and leaves but gold-tipped cigarettes already wrapped, touched with the tips of real plastic lighters.

I must say I feel safe with these men with their lighters and gold-tipped smokes. Cigarettes will back off a big lizard. I have seen it. The man with the map on his back took what was left of my page and the leaves that were burning and pointed it, stuck it right into the face of the animal as it cleared its throat coming at us, getting big with the air it inhaled, swelling up to scare us. So I'm comforted with so many of these lit tips.

The one sitting beside me smiles again. He says he knows who we are or thinks so and mouths CIA and points to himself in camaraderie. He has all his teeth when he smiles which is also camaraderie. Spears are better, he says, pointing at his weapons which I am looking at because I am tired of not looking, pretending it is nothing. The spear, he says, takes the anger into itself and when the anger is thrown, the anger finishes, and not necessarily the person. Not like with this gun, with only the trigger. With this weapon, he says, there is nowhere left for the anger to go. Only to the place to get more bullets.

I nod and let my head rest on the haft of the weapon that is just beside me. Behind his grin with all the teeth and the way he watches us as if we were a prize he had to keep from getting more valuable, is compassion which I think is unusual with someone who is in camaraderie with the CIA, at least my idea of the CIA. I nod again to give my approval more goose but the man is talking now in a language I don't know to someone else, and not even the man who is with me knows it but I hear him trying to, interrupting.

I go down to the river to get away. The river is close again this part of the driving. I'm sick in it, but that's usual. I start to wade in further to have enough water to splash and rinse off with and squat to do the insides of my legs where what I have used as a sort of bandage has leaked.

This is when I get shot.

Now getting shot isn't always lead through skin. It is also past the skin too close. Shot at. So it is not me who is bleeding into the water at my feet, though I think so, I very much think so, it is not me who flips in the water, causing the water to foam with blood, making a sound as loud as a shout but later. But not a lot later.

I get out.

Everyone should be asking if I am fine. Everyone should be asking, but they are looking at the water and pointing and not looking at me.

I turn and look where they look. It is a big animal, bigger than any I see playing with young that run like dogs in the sand. I only know its size by how long it takes for the tail to sink under the other shots, the ones that follow.

But what I see in my head is me, only shaky because my arms and legs won't be as calm as this seeing. I am separate from myself in this seeing, I am both standing in the water and here on the bank, watching as the others crowd the water. Who shot that first shot? I say, to get those two of me together. But it is as if I am not saying it. It is as if I am not there on the bank, because no one answers. They are watching the water too closely, and he is already walking back to the truck.

I could have been shot, I say when we're again sitting on the animal.

You have to be more careful, says the man who has measured my neck, the man with the nail in his lip, the man I am with.

■

We jolt forward and down in a way my stomach can't stand, like sailing far right and far left in waves of water, the way the dirt has dried in mud waves. We go against all the waves or maybe it's just that the wheels haven't enough air to make them round as we go forward, as we jolt against the waves. This is a ride that should be over in just a few hours and interesting, but this jolting has gone beyond these hours, beyond and beyond hours and interesting, gone beyond ride 'em cowboy or sailor. I bleed as we jolt and my stomach turns even when we stop.

Now we jolt and then stop, jolt and stop. What flashes metal at the end of the weapons upright in the back with us and the animal just misses me, not all at once but between stops, in between jolts.

What makes the jolts stop is a snake. The snake slithers off from where it is in the ruts where the jolts stop. Snakes are all poisonous to the people who live here no matter what color or pattern, and when I see how the snake is of a size, and how the road which we are on which is not a road is coiling like it, I am happy when the snake goes straight and away. They can't all be poisonous but they do eat what we eat which is a problem. But the truck isn't happy, the lackey inside at the wheel moves the truck after it, then stops and jolts again and the weapons in back stab at the air but not always.

I am the one who pounds. I pound on the cab like it is a skull. I pound with my fists, I say Stop. Then I don't do this alone, he does it too, the man who is with me, and they stop.

He takes someone's weapon while I talk too fast. He just takes it.

The CIA, says the man with all the teeth, again smiling. The others make wrinkles in their foreheads, either about someone with one of their guns or the snake that could crawl up the truck, I suppose, when it's stopped. There are not these wrinkles when the problem is the truck jolting. Neither the lackey nor the man with the metal who is sitting in the cab get out to see to the snake problem, however. Are they frightened of the snake or of the man with the gun who is now standing outside the truck, pointing it?

He shoots the snake. I have never seen him shoot. The long snake rises off the ground with so many bullets in its back, it reflexes in a writhe and then rolls. I writhe without thinking about how I could be it, with my back, or I think about that a little bit, but after the writhe starts.

He hands the weapon back and the long snake, with so many bullets in its back, writhes off, it reflexes and rolls. He hands the weapon back and makes a cross out of some weeds and sticks and puts in in the ground. So we won't be back, he says.

Anger is not what I guess they will break into, but it is. The snake has a spirit, even the CIA man says, and the spirit will get us. No one is happy with this killing except the man I am with and he is the one they are unhappy with, not the snake tightening and untightening muscles. They are not happy. They wanted the snake to die under the wheels so no one would do it, just the truck. I say, But the gun did it. And they shake their heads, Bad luck, Bad luck.

We are soon back to see it, we come back to the snake and its cross four more times because the road curves and loses the river, the road loses itself as dusk gathers, and can't be straight. The snake is on the way to getting there, that's for sure, since nothing's where we are, but four more times we see the snake and we stop. Four more times Bad luck, and on the last, we stop and smoke.

Even the truck smokes. We are so far from the river, riding on this snake's back in circles, that we can't put water in, we must let the truck cool. We look at each other because who will get out, just in case someone must walk to get water? We all look.

Night doesn't fall here like feathers, a little dark at a time. It attends, it groups and gathers like there's a secret that can't be let out except with a crash. That is why the people who live here put their heads under their arms at night, even here, with weapons. Weapons put into this black will stop what? Not the dark. The clouds that all day have kept the horizon dark get swallowed up by this real dark so quickly it could be rain.

We are not with a camp-out set. The ones with the guns heft them for arm rests and look out. Nothing but a firefly helps here before some real night light comes on in hours, the moon, because you can't keep the headlights on, no, not all night, if you expect to go forward into the light in the morning. So they light cigarettes which they could put into the face of something.

It is not quite dark, the best time for fear. No one gets down, not even to pee. They smoke and look away from the snake in the dark marked by the cross and talk loud against the whispers that the darkness brings out among them. Between the puffs of angry smoke that rise from the truck, the man I am with says he knows if they look at the stars, the stars will show the way. They are not hopeful. The snake is still moving, sometimes moving toward us, or toward its brother, they say, its many brothers. With its brothers, the snake will make an end to someone with as quick a revenge as this weapon had with so many bullets, they say.

It is revenge that I am planning, and maybe the others plan too. What shall it be for this man who knows so much? Surprise? Surprise, I know I am your cover, or Surprise, I am not pregnant? He must know both. His knowing does not unplan revenge however. Poison is what women use. Who would point if a CIA person drinks poison in his soup? But first there must be soup. Even poison's a food, something you put inside. I'm hungry again, just thinking of poison as food.

Already I can see the boat, its half-peanut shell filled, and me as a mourner, sitting in back, fanning away smell.

What are you thinking? he asks out of the dark, waiting for clouds to part.

I squirm. I elbow him somewhere. About the deer that's still hot. About the dark, I say. How sensual it is, a fat you can't fry.

If you have to be sick, there are always reasons. Flies, or men with their mouths open, or a liver, the best part, with worms. Cooked worms though. The question Why? is not so important as how far back the Why goes. Then you can tell when the Why should be finished or if it is going into some new Why that is different, that is worse. Say you start sick early but you don't mind, it's part of the way you are living and it's not a fever, so what? Say it gets hard to get to the river on time, to make the leaving all right and without people looking, and then you walk all day with the belly tight and then not, all cramped. Say it doesn't keep you up all night, then it does.

All night is not so bad, you say. I mean it's bad but not as bad as no place to sleep, and rain. Put the rain in, in drops as big as blood drops, drops that make noise dropping. Then get left behind because of anger at the person who separated the snake from its spirit so the truck had to wander in the snake's way, and not gratefulness at how the stars he knew made the snake stop and straighten out.

We are dropped off where there are places to stay, but in the night no one comes out to say where because of the dark. We look for a place that no one is in without going in, that is, a place with only part of a roof where no one would go. A desk is inside the one we find, with an all mud floor under it and mud walls that don't meet above, a desk which has no reason to be there but for our sleeping under it we decide. We put a skin under its legs, away from the drops that are starting to pound, to make mud. And he sleeps through the drops and the mud and the smell of the roasting which is strong even with their fire so far away.

In the night when you are sick, you don't sleep, you go out. The rain is out there, yes, and this is good. It washes the sickness, it makes it easy to clean. But there is no dryness anywhere then, not even under the desk because you bring the wetness in, because the drops collect that fall through the roof and start running under it.

Still, you don't get up when the bugs come, when light thrusts down in shafts from the no-roof part, even when some animal moves quite near you and it isn't him, he leaves because you smell, he says. He takes his pack. You sleep on and the half peanut shell with his body in it smells too, the sleep is so solid. All of what was inside is forgotten by what held it, all but the bleeding which he knows about. He must know about it now.

Because it is increasing. The increase is hard to hide even with inside and outside protection and the disposing of this protection so no child will use it in something he is doing because it is not what he knows. And it is hard to find enough excuses to keep him from entering me. Not that he's asked in the rain of that night. Or is he noticing me more than I think? He is watching me more. That's what I think but I am not sure. I know he doesn't like sick, sick is too close to death and death is too much his friend as he says in his sleep so often I think he is awake saying it.

I have never lost so much blood. It can't be the meat I am not eating that makes it so red. I lie on the ground so the ground takes the blood, and I rest and think about meat, the stew you could make from the animal we sat on and how it is probably finished. I try to close my eyes to make it more real but my stomach keeps them open. And the sound.

A long *a* sound with little breath between *a*'s is said by many somewhere outside, not too far outside. The voices are not all young but some are, I think, many are. I hear the different sounds of the *a*, even though the sound itself is mad. It begins again, and a man passes the door that is so broken down it has a hole that you do not have to crouch through, convenient in the night for me, and this man, of whom I can see just the bottom half, has chains all around what he's not wearing, even on his wrists, which he swings as he paces, which he does in front of my door twice, and then passes. So I see what mad is, and how even here with the fresh air and no traffic and deadlines, even here with its dying and disease and snakes, someone could go mad and I'm comforted, not having just made it up for myself.

Then the *b* begins. All the voices together, altogether like a stutterer's, all those different attacks. And I don't even have to move to know that madness isn't for me today at all, that it can't be, there is this *b*.

The alphabet is quite a comfort. I sleep with the inevitable rhythm of the rest, the other twenty-odd coming, promising no surprise. I don't need surprise. I need rest instead, and when I look next, one of the alphabeteers has slipped inside, two of them. They look at me with looks that show I am their surprise, the way, in a book, small people tie up a big one with a kingdom at stake. You know, a satire. I hold out my hand to see if I am cold against one of their hands, and, of course, to feel the touch of someone. They look at each other and decide against this touch. They pick up both ends of the desk that is still over me and lift it away, though they are not the size to do it. They take it out the door, lifting and pushing.

I want to stop them and have them say their long *a*'s for me and then their *b*'s, but I can't think of anything but Charlies. I know that Charlie is probably a word they use because they are in school, in fact the school I am in, but I am too tired to think of what to put with Charlie or to move. I let the blood go into the ground. I sleep again.

■

He is holding me up now. I must look like I need it, and I must say it is hard to hold myself up. He gives me a drink of water and all the time I am drinking I think how I must move away from him, I must get away. Did you see some blue people? I ask while I move a little away from him, while I fix myself.

We have to go a little farther.

I sink back, as much as you can when you're sunk already. How far?

An Arab, he says, has breakfast. Maybe he knows.

He helps me up, we walk along, me like I have a broken leg or at least a sprain because I can't go at a pace, I have time to get stickers in my feet that hurt, and think. Before, when I walked fast and skimmed them, they brushed off my feet. I never worried. Now I move onto them and they ease straight into my footskin and hurt. Like my thoughts.

We take seats at the Arab's instead of skins, seats of canvas spread like a butterfly, like my mother had, a fifties sling that cuts off your line of sight if you don't sit forward, but it's comfortable. We face the river instead of each other.

Someone across the river burns dead grass and smoke rises off its bank, rises to the bottom of the heavy clouds that make a dark far off. This smoke is hope, though, not death: shoots will come up after the dew sits at night, the shoots are so ready to grow, shoots that cows can eat.

The Arab serves tea. The dead flies on top of the grey brew or the flies still swimming in the sugar at the bottom are no problem. I drink, holding the flies away from my mouth with my finger that has been washed when? I let the hot sugar and tea go all the way down with the water from the river whose bank is burning. Because of the wings of my chair I don't know if the others are drinking the same, or watching me drink. I just drink and it is like a glass of cold water this hot tea, a water I know we can't afford.

What has he used? I know my book with its last chapters is back with my pack. I always look to see its bulge, especially when he leans into his, which is what? And of course we have no more empty cassettes, those gone with the eggs, before I knew I had paper for money. Something, he pays with something.

The Arab is very thin, and the boy who is taking our glasses has whisps for fingers and I can't see the skeleton under the dress that they wear but the boy's head is a little too big for the quickness of his eyes, and the way he licks the inside of my glass before the flies do I don't want to see. But while the Arab's thinness seems all tired, the boy's lively, inside-the-eyes thinness is different. I lean forward past the wings to see more, and cramp.

The tired Arab has a cassette and is slipping it into his sleeve where, I don't know, money would go. His hands are spotted. Blue? It is like blue but more purple on his almost-my-color skin. I wonder at the color but I am too weak to lean forward again, and anyway this clenching somewhere around the stomach but not the stomach is bad. The tea? Poison?

I am ungrateful, he says, as he helps me back. So what if I used one of your cassettes. You have plenty of songs.

I am quiet. I can't talk and walk at the same time but he doesn't know that yet. He just knows walking is hard because of how I spent the night.

I could be sick too, he says.

I know what he means.

■

I have not mentioned my name: Good For Nothing. The why of it is how the grain fell when I put the pestle in once, and how I have the wrong skin for this sun, and how once I put my clamshell back into the pot which is like spitting, and yes, how I can't get water to stay in the vessel that I can almost balance on my head but not walk with. It also means silly. I like silly. I try for silly. When people laugh, I am not nothing then, I am good.

This man with sunglasses wants to change the name. First he says he will marry me with cows in England for my father's cows. This is in an accent which is King James: We will converse together, he says. I didn't hear him speak on the ride in the truck but his sunglasses say educated and sexy together and even when it is pitch dark like inside this place they stay on. Because of malaria I think, those terrible yellow eyes, or eyes that are crossed. It can't be only educated and sexy.

Spies, he says when he collects us after the tea. They go to Arabs.

I now sit on a cot off the floor and I can swing my legs in the air and my bottom fits on it in a soft wedge. I have been sleeping since he led us here, in custody, he said, me being so happy for custody. But when a cigarette comes on in the black, I sit up, or try to.

You think I'm a CIA woman, I say. You think I am for anyone.

You are not married, he says.

I am a woman, I say, and my guts clench.

He pulls on the gold-tipped cigarette so smoke whitens the darkness between us. You have done a big thing, this changing of our songs to yours. You need a new name.

I do, I say. I am dumb with his saying so and why. I almost cry out Yes but I think he is listening, this man who is asleep beside me, so I say I do again.

My time for not speaking is over.

He gets up, still smoking. His cigarette and the dark shape of him pass the cot that the man I am with sleeps on, is sleeping on, whose toes face my face, the cots are so tight in this space, and he leaves.

From inside, I hear the bleats outside. I pull myself to the edge of the cot and look out where the door is now pushed to the floor like a window. In this *u* of light, I see him with a goat on a rope and a spear in his hand that he must have taken from the cook, a long-bladed spear with a shaft as tall as he is, this man with the cigarette, the red of the gold tip showing around that shaft where the cigarette is still burning in his hand.

You are no longer Good for Nothing, he says into the air and at the goat, You are Daughter of the Nile. And, glancing over to where my face must show through the hole in the door, he plunges the spear with force into the little kid's neck, the long part that you would cover with covers if it were a child in bed.

He steps back.

The kid doesn't empty out right, doesn't twitch and roll eyes and gasp to limpness. Its hooves rush and the head swivels back as if to breathe better, its breath bubbles with the blood coming out at the neck. The man places his cigarette in a woven part of the wall of the place behind him and does not smile. He steps toward the kid again, lifts the head by the ears and saws at the neck with the blade end, a not-so-sharp blade that the skin follows back and forth.

Goat man, he says, the man who was asleep but who is not at the door with me. Oh, goat man of the politic spear, he sings, as if he were one of the people, this man's people. You can't change her name, killing like that.

Ah, the CIA is here, the man finishing the goat sings back. The CIA who knows just how to do this.

This is fine, I say. Thank you.

Ah, Daughter of the Nile, with her tongue always out for What is this and Charlie that, he sings, the one who is coming out behind me.

The other one doesn't look at me as if he is part of me, the one who is singing. Instead, he turns his back and takes time digging a glass out of a hole under the hood of the truck where the truck sits in the middle of the other men napping and smoking as if it is tethered, and the glass he finds comes with a bottle.

Let us drink to the woman who is Daughter of the Nile, who is saving our songs for the BBC Africa Hour, when our sons are businessmen of oil and land and want to hear in songs how big their fathers were.

I nod but I wonder.

Then we drink while the kid dies for good. What the drink is is strong, a kick in the emptiness I have for food which remembers food as a large animal tilting which is not here except in the stomachs of the weapons-bearing men with no sign of the animal ever having been what they sat on, let alone ate, though I see a dog with a long bone which cannot be the kid's that is still shaking.

The drink is clear and not much. Thank you, I say when the bottle and its glass are given to me again. Thank you for the new name. Then I hand on the glass.

No more, please.

He is draining the glass and refilling it and passing it again to the man I am with like the glass has to be drained. And from the heat that moves through me after my one glass, through and behind my ears pinching like a pair of hot earrings, I think not very much really but toward the end of song as it is known, toward some final new song that all of us will be singing.

■

Where are the rows of corn? I stare at stalks not so well woven, no, a job by someone in the night or early morning, and the stalks are not new which is right since I never see rows. It is too dry for rows of anything but the lines trucks make in the hard mud, trying to stay in a row. I am sick but the cornstalks far from their rows shelter me, though some are gone for the fire that the kid ribs are roasting on. Then I am finished with sickness or it is finished with me.

The two men are three now, the new one the man with the metal on his chest. Metal or medal? Every country has some code way of saying this is who you should look for. This man sat in the cab all the lost way, partly because of the metal and what it means, and partly because he is short and short here, with all not, is a good thing to hide if you're in charge. Even now he is sitting, his hands around the glass now grey with dust and handgrease from its passing hand to hand.

He says, Why songs? when I make my way in, close to where the kid's ribs roast over the cornstalks, with the heat and smoke in my eyes which I don't back off from because smoke is almost food. He says, Why songs? again. And then, You want to eat all of us: our dancing—and his feet make out some steps that I do for rock and roll in the dark, but without his getting up on his—our music, and his lips move in the style of a trumpet player and his hands do the drum after the notes of the trumpet—and now the very words we use that come to us in beauty, the very words you suck out and put into the throat of a machine that can't swallow because it is so full of all the other words it has taken before from others. But it will swallow, he says. In time.

The mouth of the man who changed my name does not move under its dark glasses. He has no metal on his front, just stripes. He stands straight and takes the next drink.

Oh, no, says the one who is with me. She is taking your songs so she doesn't have to sing her own. Nobody cares about your songs. She has to make them care so they will listen to her and, later, listen to her songs, when she makes them.

I can't leave. The ribs roast. I count the seven deadly sins and think of the place in the drawer where my mother keeps hankies. It's hard work, I say, Who does that for nothing?

Your people, says the man with the metal. Women.

I don't move away, I don't flinch because grease runs off the ribs into the ash in front of me.

Women, shakes the head of the man who is with me. They are free now, free not to have babies.

Is this so? asks the man with the glasses, his voice old from not being in the talking.

The question is for me. I do the least answer, I nod. I lift my chin and lower it with my head. I reach into the fire and pull at a rib in the silence but the rib doesn't come off. It's still stuck, flesh to bone.

No children? they say finally, their mouths open one at a time.

Independent, says my man. She wants to be like us.

Free for sex, says my man.

That is free, says the man with the metal. I have seen this.

I pick up the spear that still has kid blood on the blade and I raise it. The men stop passing the glass and the bottle.

The blade comes down, not with practice but desperate, it comes down on four of the ribs until the ribs graze the ashes, free. I pick them out of the ashes, I take them and eat them, and the grease runs to my elbows, runs off.

I am tired of hunger.

Every girl fears sex being handed out after every hand-shake, in fact, we wash those hands, those shakes being all the foreplay we sometimes get, we wash like boxers or golfers before bouts that just have skill at stake and no love. But it is all about love, just no one knows how to get love into those shakes or if it is there already, where exactly—

in the grip? In the air between the palms? I see this now in tonight's dark which has no TV written into the walls of its riverbank to change the subject which is the sound of his voice, which I love because there is no other?

Salt is the worst, he is saying, salt bonds the fastest. Put a piece of silver in salt and you get plate but what kind of salt? You ever think about the kind of salt you get from those silver shakers your mother moves around the table?

Silver-tongued salt, I say, but I don't say the bleeding's stopped a little. I say, Think of the bloody swamps where you grew up, that water red from the cannons coming apart in the backwater, the red iron, I say, that's what you drank. Which makes you what? You think nothing will come through you. Especially not love, I add.

He kisses me.

They say if a woman hangs around the river at night, a cannibal will come and eat her, I say.

I've always wondered about morals of stories, he says. For instance, is it moral to steal honey from bees, smoke them out of house and hive and eat their secretions? Do bees have blood or is honey blood?

It's not so bad, I say, watching dusk suck the bugs out, watching bugs so thick their wings darken the dusk more.

What? He's throwing dirtclods at hippos whose red ears twitch both in their reflection and the water. It's not so bad to eat women or honey?

It's not so bad here when all the men are naked, I say. You always know their intentions.

He hits one of the animals and it turns but when it calls out, it's to a mate.

Careful. This is not *National Geographic* where we cut to shooting behind glass somewhere, or with some long lens.

They never cut away during the mating scenes, he says. He takes me by the waist and says I'm beautiful which has to be some kind of lie but what kind? All of me sticks from dirt that comes with the honey we hunted, and my hair's matted from so many no-soap washings, and my bones show. In this light I could only be skinny.

He feels me all over which I don't resist because I am tired. I struggle with bugs instead of his hardness.

The hippos float off in a light stain of red. He says without saying anything about the red, Sometimes babies are born here with teeth or who can talk. They tell the future, both of them, he says. I saw signs in the capitol once, Right this way. The baby made a fortune.

The language has an open *o*, I say, a sound babies can make. I don't say, Read the river, see the red, I'm not bearing you into the future, saving you from certain death.

I say, What did you see?

A baby, he says, throwing another clod. It was asleep. It was so cute. He puts his head on his hand and tucks it under my hand.

I push him away.

I start back to what? A small mound of belongings in front of a doorway.

He follows, he follows too close. I hurry away from his head and his hands as best I can with new cramps. He is whispering things, a kind of hissing which I can't understand, it is not in the language I know or the one I speak with him. Maybe he can tell the future, maybe he's that kind of baby.

Beside the mound of belongings sit two women. I'm not that sick I say, seeing what they are doing.

He stands beside me. Look, it's not so bad, he says, they don't even make noise.

He means moans. The flies that like the blood lick at it as it runs off, they lick so much she twitches, so much you can hear the licks go fast when a new stripe goes down.

The flies don't bother the cutter. She is pressing down in the middle of the head where he has told me sickness is always thought to be staying.

I feel sick but not that sick. I don't mind blood, it can rush out or stay. It's the razor sound I mind, not the sharpness, or its lack, the razor tip as it pulls through, that sound. And the flies. Maybe you could catch things from them, I say, but the flies don't move and spread themselves around. They like licking more than they like flying.

He says, Feeling better already?

I look at the cutter who puts a horn on the head and sucks. What does she have that needs so much curing? is my question.

What is it that women want most? he says. What is it here, at least?

I don't say Babies.

There is only one thing I want, I say. I walk, a little two-mile walk, like the Arab said, two miles to the blue people. It will make a difference, I say. What I don't say is, This is a test: If you are a spy, you will want to go home because you've done what you need to do, what you are paid to do, with the cassette, and measuring and talking. If you are not, you will walk, and shoot.

We're not going, he says. Look at you—you're so pale, I can see the dark through you.

It's a new kind of suntan.

What I want to say is What a good girl I am, please don't kill me, I've gone to communion and knelt to get my throat blessed, this uncut throat, and I've fasted for the saint who was stabbed for only singing to virgins and though I did run away at music camp with an oboist who could kiss, I didn't with a man with an all-over suntan at a hotel.

I don't hear the way he says how I don't look so well because I will hear where there is caring which I can't hear now, I can't take that out and hear it.

It's only two miles away, I say.

You shoot, he says, if it's so easy, you shoot.

And he leaves, goes away from the mouth of our place, in the direction of the camp because we are not far away now, just a few cornstalk fences, and one of the paths leads to where the Arab says the blue people live, but not the one he turns on, the one that ends on men who are not like him and do not know how he should act, so he likes to be there.

I turn my back on the woman who is sick and her cutter, and go into his pack. My knowing must be now.

The lump is a camera that makes pictures as soon as you shoot, with a gun grip. It is not a gun but it is like a gun in what the pictures from it say. Flat and sticky to the side lie these pictures in a wad with the results so bad I think first how can he be a person to put a whole people in boxes with a camera? The pictures are all empty, all almost white framed-in-white. But with a second look, seeing the little

wiggles of his writing here and there not writing with letters but numbers, I think they show who he is.

I take the camera. All good campers leave with everything they come with, but exposed. I will come back with
pictures he can't refuse to see, to look at with his shooting.
I want to make him do this, to prove he is not what the
pictures say he is. After all, it is his cover—why not shoot
his cover? It feels crazy but the dark as it darkens with me
in it, alone, and my cramps and the no food makes the
crazy okay, fine.

To walk in the dark is not crazy, I say out loud, after it is
too dark to do anything but pack the pack. I wait such a
long time in case he comes back that the spot in the front
where the woman sat who is now gone, is just a place with
flies in the dark. I put the door to the place in place behind
that spot.

The dark is cool, the pain in my gut doesn't press so hard
in the night, and in dark as black as this, I can think other
people walk with me, people from where you offer your
wrists and they pull out the blood in tubes. And I know the
path, it begins just after the cornstalk lean-to, where the
press of the feet goes on, where they have made a rut for a
middle, a place smooth, a bottom-of-a-boat place.

Most animals in the dark don't trouble another that is
moving. That's the last thing I decide, shifting the camera
to under the arm where it doesn't bump and make noise.
Animals are not trouble because most animals that feed in
the dark look for animals that are sleeping then, sure
things. The competition is walking around in the dark, no
animal another of these animals wants to meet. I think.

It's not so dark. Lightning chops at the tops of the clouds

that pile up over the black that I walk under but so far away it could be long tubes of light from buildings that never turn them off, even when morning's coming. It's so late or early, no one is watching, so there's no man with a gun at the edge of the camp asking Where and Why. He has had his drink or still drinks it.

I walk two hours. Two miles in two hours is the wrong time, even with pain in the gut. The path curves far right or left in ways I don't understand, point to point being the reason for a path, the philosophy of path, pathness. But there are always other reasons here, not just my reasons.

Once I hear things. Since I cannot see, hearing is what I do between lightnings. I hear someone coming after me which I expect even if the man with the gun at the edge of the camp has had his drink. But I am not worried, as long as it is a someone and not a thing, an animal. Then I don't hear the sound. This could mean someone was just coming out to do something alone, without the cornstalk lean-to, walking as far as he can to do it.

I walk on, without stopping. The people who walk with me in the thick of this dark are women, mothers maybe, with shields, women let out of zoos where people point and say, There's one who wasn't a man and did this, how quaint. But I'm not the one to shoot and I have enough songs, he's right. I say Tomorrow—if the blue people aren't right—I'll go. No problem, they answer in my skin, in my walk which keeps on.

I time my leaving so the sun will rise when I walk in. But with two miles in two hours I am late. I enter blinking.

Maybe the English thought of somewhere else here which is why the stumps of the trees in two rows leading from the town to the river are so broad and well spaced. A walk from the river to the town under these leaves that are now fuel could make you pretend that, and the hole with cement steps in and out could be a pool next to the courts which have lines that are all faded, with cement buckled in wide cracks under these faded lines. I would like to lie in that pool beside those courts and not be bitten by bugs nor set upon by those who find a woman in the day without all the clothes that a day needs on her, and there I would drink to the English something English in that place.

But the pool needs covering.

As I stand by the pool, someone comes and puts another blue one in.

Color, fixed in black, lies. A blue could be purple or even brown, on black, especially when it is not an all-over blue, especially when it is not a pool-blue. The color of this pool is not blue except for the blue that is put in which is not a reflection of the kind of sky here. The blue ones are put in the pool because the ground is too hard to dig.

Beside the pool, horns go through the fence of the court, offerings of what is the best here to offer, with the skins of cats, small and spotted to match the stars they move under, the ones that fade so quickly as I approach this place, as the sky goes from pale to blue. These skins are woven in around the horns as charms. One set of horns has a head that I remember, but do animals with the same stripes and horns all look the same? My head in a row would just say *female* under it, the way these in the pool who are blue just say *human*.

I am looking into this pool but also smelling it, with flies, with birds, with lime that eats with the others. The animals that lope dog-like but rocking stay away while I stand and smell.

A whole place can stop having people. The blue spots on the skin that are purple on another color skin will do it, although men here do not enter men to get blue because here men enter women to live forever, to get children from women who are nothing without them. But they get this blue anyway, with or without men on men.

The children. None of them sitting by the side of the pool or sorting through the bundles of, and bags of, boxes that lie scattered in an exploded way which is how the air lets bundles and bags down from planes, are old enough to be marked with the cuts across the head which say you can have sex or war. None of the children are blue. They must not be born blue nor be old enough to get blue.

They don't come around me like they do wherever I go, to laugh at my speaking. They sit in piles by the bundles and bags and boxes by the pool. One of the blue ones in the pool must be someone for them, probably more than one.

I walk to the end of the pool, past the court, past the fence. The wall here has a chart of the insides of a woman on it, with the letters *U.N.* under that, and a hoop is screwed on over the chart, a hoop with string coming apart from its edges. Someone screwed in that hoop after the English, someone with charts and balls to bounce. But that someone has left.

It is a camp-like place when I turn around a little to look everywhere, a place that needs only wires and dogs and guns around it to say Do Not Enter or Go. I have seen pictures of these places and the teeth that are left after.

A child, stoning the birds that drift down, stops and

comes toward me. I take a picture of him just as he finds the strength to move off, squirting offal behind him.

The blue turns almost black except for close-ups, one close-up of someone who stops his chest from rising up and down just after, whose woman holding him crosses his hands over this chest after, and does not speak. I do not put the picture up in front of her to give to her because in it, the chest is also stopped. I put it where my shirt goes into my skirt, against my skin with the other pictures so my hands are free. For what? To ward off what?

The path is not where it was after I block my sight with the camera, and seeing the man whose chest stopped. I am turning for it, turning, when a man makes his way to me with a syringe bearing something dark inside that drips out. He wants me to make a hole in his arm and put the dark inside. *Booma*, he says. It will make him strong. He raises his blue stick arm.

You would think that horror would make your legs work fast unless it is a dream horror and your legs can't move or move in honey, slow and thick, the horror getting closer. When I find the path, I run but I can't, even without a dream. Run is not much of a word for what I do. My cramps and fear fill in where the run would be.

I walk, I stagger, I walk. Where this place ends, past the pool, a child offers me bread from a bundle, from a bag. We have food, she says. We are not hungry.

It takes two hours for two miles and the high grass which slaps my legs in the dawn is now sharp and cuts, and my gut tightens and cuts, and I can't see over the grass to know exactly where the river is or could be or any other paths. I know the cornstalk lean-to is the end, though when I see it, it leans badly, leans almost over, and animals crawl out as I push in.

The stalks sway when I push in, they almost fall but I am finished with the worry that someone will see me. Someone should see me—and see the blue people too. I stare up into the blue where the cornstalks don't come together and all of me empties, comes apart into a hole nearly too full to take more while the twists in my gut get harder, they press into the gut without me pressing.

I keep staring up in case an airplane puts its white slash across this hole but I know that is silly to watch for, no one is coming to save me when a whole place is dying with no one to save it. Certainly not the men with guns.

I put those last words out into the air one at a time, between breaths, the words meaning nothing but a chant I make, my guts coming out as they come. I breath these words and then look.

Out of me comes a white lump and its dropping makes the overflow, and a heavy sound as it sinks in.

I cry.

We are not going to the blue people, says the man with the metal. The last time we came, they shot at us and I know from today they have new weapons and ammo. Maybe we'll come back after the rains.

The man who thinks he is just like us makes his smile. He has not been at the camp since the night we came in the rain. It is his report of new weapons.

I lie at the back of the place, draining into the ground. Who shot at who?—Is the color blue new?—Is that the weapon?—Is what I don't say.

They do not know I know. My being gone is answered by what happened, is happening now, into the ground. The man who is with me is not holding my hand, if he would hold it, because his is cuffed. He is cuffed for saying Nigger last night and almost fighting. I don't know what about. I have never seen men fight except for play on the streets. This might be play unless the man with the metal just wants me to stay with this man and not go on with them.

The man with the metal pops the buttons on our cassette player in stacatto, impatient with him in his cuffs and me, and the journey they made and the one that they face. The truck in front of us is almost full. The men with their weapons shift them like they are extra now and not part of their arms or legs, and a few droop. In disappointment?

He is not saying yet whether we are returning with him or not. The man with the smile is unspooling all the film into the sun and looking at it. Unspooling it like that makes it all black whether or not it has a picture on it. He peers at it as if there are things to see which is what I wish, even if now the sun takes them back. Can after can come unsealed and cool air from where they are sealed must rush out, though I'm too far away to feel it. The man in the cuffs looks as if he has never looked to put people together in the box that the camera makes, but he does look away. Fury at the waste? Or his cover uncovered?

Soon there are just tails, no more film left in any can, just a paper that says anything can be shot, with signatures on it. This paper the man turns upsidedown and does not read because upsidedown, who can read it?—but he looks at it upsidedown with his lips pressed tight and then he places it very carefully in the hand of the man with the metal.

The motor goes on in the vehicle we came in while the man with the metal reads, while he tears it up. Exhaust plumes into the gold light of the morning that is half over, plumes up past the falling paper, past the door to the cab that is just now cracked open. The woman in here, says the man with the metal, the man in back.

The woman who does want children, he says, in a kind kind of voice while he moves to the middle so I have air at the window. Every six months, he says to me as the truck moves away from this place, every six months I go to lay with my wife who is twelve hundred and sixty-five miles away. And every three months after this laying, she makes what you have, for nothing. I will soon divorce her.

What he says sounds decided at the beginning then drops at the end in a question, something that is hard to decide, or something that I am not supposed to hear.

At least you are not yet blue, I say.

He does not look at me but at the machine that plays our cassettes in his lap. He says, It is a place that they make to get rid of sick people. I am supposed to get rid of them, for myself and for the land. This is the third time I make this trip and I am supposed to do it, for the good of our people.

I grip the seat to keep from hitting my head on the dash in the bumps, the ones that are not so hard now that the rain has beat down once or twice before the sun comes,

I get a grip on the seat's vinyl to keep from jolting out more blood.

The man you are with does not seem too sad over the film that we take out. He has more somewhere else?

I smile. It's a foolish kind of smile that will get you into certain troubles quickly if you don't move it into something rueful soon. I lean forward over my gut, feeling the pictures in my shirt, and I say I'd be the last to know. Then I faint which is what you do if you haven't had much sleep on top of food and this blood problem.

■

The sun is shining terribly when I wake up, shining through the clouds in swords that pool in spots where, if someone stood in one, they would go straight up into the clouds, into a spaceship or a chariot or a plane or else get lasered into meat for stepping into the light. There's no avoiding them, though the lackey seems to try. I wake because we swing wildly between light spots and great swags of water that are caught deep in mud, lake-fat from rain. The truck slides between the light and the mud, then dives into the river that is in the way, an arm of the river that has grown with the rain into a whole limb that we have to cross anyway. Even the lackey leaves the cab then, leaving just me inside with my not walking, even the man I am with, in his cuffs, wades outside.

He wasn't back from the camp when I crawled in, so dirty and wet and weak. He saw the dirt and the wet and blood I smeared over what we had since there was nothing else to use and said nothing because it looked like anger.

Or crazy. But then I tell him. I tell him because I want him to know what I have done for him, and to make him unhappy.

His answer is only that I am not strong enough now, like I am some kind of animal that, with better hay, will improve, like this is only the first time.

No thanks, I say.

The river pushes against the truck as hard as the hands that push it back, although everyone pushes hard so the truck doesn't follow the river into where it swells. In the pushing, the river comes up to my window, seeps in under my legs, washes at the red that I leave on the seat if I move. The river washes in more.

The man with the dark glasses pulls me out through the window, carries me across, though his gun gets wet and maybe I stain him. He sets me down flat to the ground like wood that doesn't float, then he turns away fast to help the truck back.

■

They take apart the truck to dry, so dry, it might run. The sun does dry well this time of day in its swords from the clouds. I lay on my back facing the sun, one arm up and then the other, and soon I am dry where the tips were wet. The man I am with, with his hands cuffed, sits at my side and tells me a story.

Once, when he was here before, he says, we had a jeep. We went across a river like this, very much like this only not here, to get a suitcase of the stuff that I like. On the way back, when we had already smoked some of what the suitcase held, we found a straight, flat patch to drive fast over, with no bumps. We were driving fast this way when five men with machine guns came out, a lot like the way the giraffes came out, out of nothing, remember? And the leader of the men gave me a paper which had writing on it: We will kill you.

I gave the paper to the man who was driving, the man who was a brother to someone with one of the guns, or at least I hoped so, and he talked very fast because what else could he do? They talked back and smiled and nodded and pointed at their guns and I said What? What? And they smiled more and pointed at the guns and said, We will kill you.

You're not dead, I say.

I can't look at him.

We could have killed you is what they meant. They hadn't learned the conditional when the war broke out. We should have warned them we were coming across their flat patch.

We could have killed you, he says again.

That means the danger is over? I ask. If I just say the right thing?

You're so pale, he says, and walks away.

Pale is the death that he hates as if it is something that is catching, surely an instinct left from when people had no idea about whether it was caught or not. But who can blame him?

Me. I doze, which is like fainting in the sun, now.

■

I keep the pictures under my shirt. No one is taking the shirt off now. My bed under the net is my bed and I can see the lump in my pack that is my book the same size as the truck which is driving off. He is bigger than the truck because he is not in it, he does not need cuffs here, or them to keep him, there is rain to keep him, a rain that covers the back of the truck with its men and weapons so quickly as it leaves it could be gate. He would have the pictures himself if he saw them but he is standing there, not looking at me which is fine.

The dog is not fine. The dog walked out when the truck drove up, he walked, and did not bound or bark.

He is not starving, I say. The dog is round in the right places and his feet are bigger. I try to see more of him from my flat place, and fail. It is the breathing that says the dog is not fine, a sound of ripping.

■

If you lie in moonlight, it is bad luck. My eyes are open in the moonlight because I am finished sleeping and the moonlight is cutting across my place to his, in one white finger. I should wake him, hearing this breathing, but I don't.

Hymns hum through the dark, but the baby boys and silence and manger are not right for the sound of the voices in that language but probably as right as the way I make their songs in reverse, probably just as right. But it can't be Christmas. No radio says no though. It does rain now where once it was dry, and I have walked and walked. Maybe they are just singing what they know or I am dreaming in this unlucky light, this light that doesn't touch me.

Bottles of 23 stick up and around the light. He was sick, the one who liked these, the one who left. The one whose subject was blue people, who liked women, who was sick how? Was he blue?

The dog breathes badly.

■

You kill him.

I turn my face so it is not in any direction of his.

You have killed before.

He means the lump that I lost, in hunger and sickness.

Killed? I shout. It is hard for me to shout No without losing more of myself, but the No must be shouted because the rain is so loud, it beats. This shouting will kill me, I shout.

Here. He has a syringe and he fills it with rain water.

The dog moans and wags and comes for it, and he sluices the water down the dog's throat. The dog thumps and moves his front paws and rocks his head. He has not had water for some time, even though the water is right there, the rain is coming down. He can't swallow or breath now. Now he moves his tongue in and out with the water.

Now a pink piece of flesh slides out and onto the ground.

The dog makes better breathing sounds as if the tongue had been the problem all along, as if it were in the way of breathing, the dog paws toward me where he has tossed the syringe, for more. I see this in a shadow, I hear it in the slobbery way it comes toward me, louder.

Please, I say.

Sit up, he says. Roll over. Confess.

To one side of me leans a tripod and that's all. I raise myself on my arm and pull it down, I heave it and pull the heavy head of the tripod down.

The dog dies without moving or making a whine.

The dog stays there, a little blood from his head going into the dirt like mine until he picks up the front paws and pulls it out into the rain, whistling like he knew I would do it.

■

She comes. It is after I have given up getting up. I can't. I am still alive but I can't. She says the man with the metal has sent her because it is not a good idea to have a white woman die in this place. What about blue women? I am too weak to ask.

She gives me a pill she has tied up in a cloth, a brown pill the size and color of my nipples that stay brown. She says it is from the missionary's.

I take it dry, like communion, I put up saliva to take it inside me where the bleeding is, where another woman's bleeding is what I replace. I don't ask who can spare it on the long line of waiting in sun that would kill me. I take it.

But she is not finished with just the pill. She pushes at my belly with her hands at whatever soft thing is inside it still, she pushes and I yell, not because I hurt, but because I am afraid more blood will come out and I am trying hard to keep it in which doesn't work. She keeps pushing and more blood comes out, but I am better with her warm hands on me. For these warm hands, I stop looking at the top of the place we are in and at her.

Maybe her skin is black. I don't see it. I see dark eyes and knitted brows and pursed lips. I see I am a body in her hands, a body she warms.

I let her find the pictures under my shirt. She stares at them, then speaks too quickly or maybe in Arabic so I don't understand. She shakes her head. But I can see by how long she looks at the picture she doesn't know who or what or she thinks she knows but their thinness won't say Yes, this is me, this is your cousin or uncle. I shake my head back. She gives them back.

She has something knotted somewhere below where I can see which she brings up and opens.

A nail. Just a nail. It is not a nail with a name, a finishing one or a hobnail, but it is not too small so it would be mistaken for a pin. The sun from the open door is on it and whitens it to small sword.

I have no money to buy it, I say. But it isn't true. I have my half a book in a bag under my head. I want to tell her I am not someone who wants to take from her, even with money. I want to thank her. Look at my nipples, they are still brown I want to say, but the words are too much for me. I close my eyes. I have no money because I am doing you the favor of leaving as soon as my blood and the rains stop.

She says it is his.

I don't understand. I don't understand when she says this was what they took from the river. And I don't understand that this is all I have, just this piece, just this nail from his lip that was inside of the stomach he was found in.

He was returning from finding me, she says. The man with the metal says Yes, I live here, and this man you are with goes to find me. I was behind him when it gets him but I get out.

Then she leaves me with the nail.

I want to tell him I must have wanted it, not like a victim who wants to be a victim but as a kind of cement that would make whatever he was and was not doing go away.

Be dead and get it over with.

I say this to him in the air that is left after she goes away, the gold air, even though I know this air is not the air you can breathe always, breath after breath.